BT

'We did. We make a good team.'

'Hell, yes. A damned fine team. Like a well-oiled machine.'

His lips curved into a grin that she suddenly wanted to kiss.

No. She couldn't. They'd agreed not to get involved. Especially not when there was a child involved. Too much to want. Too much to leave. Too much potential for fresh hurt.

But she couldn't help feeling pride at his compliments. He made her feel respected. Valued. He took time out to talk to her, to thank her for the small things. And the fire in his eyes made her feel desirable for the first time in for ever.

He was starting to make her feel things—and she didn't want to feel at all. Her palm rested briefly over her stomach, felt the dips and ridges of her scars. Remembered the pain she'd endured and survived. She'd felt enough to last her a lifetime.

Dear Reader

This is my debut novel for Mills and Boon® Medical Romance™, and I'm thrilled you've picked up a copy!

This story is set in North Beach, a fictional place based on the many beautiful townships dotted around coastal New Zealand. The sparkling ocean, white sand and friendly community offer a haven of tranquillity.

For Jessie and Luke North Beach also offers a fabulous place to heal a broken heart—although they're both too stubborn to realise it.

We all have our fantasies of how our happy-ever-after will be. But for Jessie and Luke past experiences have tainted their ideals. They've both experienced loss and abandonment, and neither is looking for love.

While writing this I wanted to explore themes of hope in the face of tragedy, and to examine what *family* means. Is it purely flesh and blood? Or is it forged from the emotional ties that bind us?

I hope you enjoy Jessie and Luke's journey, watching them slowly learn to trust, laugh and let in love again.

I would love to hear from you—visit me at www.louisageorge.com

Warm wishes

Louisa

ONE MONTH TO BECOME A MUM

BY
LOUISA GEORGE

First published in Great Britain 2012
by Mills & Boon, an imprint of Harlequin (UK) Limited.
Large Print edition 2012
Harlequin (UK) Limited, Eton House,
18-24 Paradise Road, Richmond, Surrey TW9 1SR

© Louisa George 2012

ISBN: 978 0 263 22473 3

Printed and bound in Great Britain
by CPI Antony Rowe, Chippenham, Wiltshire

A lifelong reader of most genres, **Louisa George** discovered romance novels later than most, but immediately fell in love with the intensity of emotion, the high drama and the family focus of Mills & Boon® Medical Romance™.

With a Bachelors Degree in Communication and a nursing qualification under her belt, writing Medical Romance seemed a natural progression—the perfect combination of her two interests. And making things up is a great way to spend the day!

An English ex-pat, Louisa now lives north of Auckland, New Zealand, with her husband, two teenage sons and two male cats. Writing romance is her opportunity to covertly inject a hefty dose of pink into her heavily testosterone-dominated household. When she's not writing or researching Louisa loves to spend time with her family and friends, enjoys travelling, and adores great food. She's also hopelessly addicted to Zumba®.

**This is Louisa's first book
for Mills & Boon® Medical Romance™.
Look out for more from her,
coming soon!**

To my Mum.
Thank you for your never-ending supply
of laughter, love and support,
and for gifting me the love of words.

For Warren, Sam and James.
You guys are my *everything*.
With you in my life
I am the luckiest woman in the world.
I love you.

CHAPTER ONE

JESSICA PRICE dived deep into her brother's backyard pool and savoured the cool water.

Heat burnt into her eyes.

Damn.

Pain stabbed behind her eyeballs.

She breaststroked to the pool edge and rubbed her face, squeezed the water from her eyes. And again. Tried to focus across the garden, but saw nothing except a series of blurred shadows. Soft edges.

Slipping out of the pool, she stumbled to the outside shower, breath stuttering as ice-cold water doused her face.

That pool should come with a health warning. She'd have to check the chemical balance before she got into it again. Tired frustration limped through her jet-lagged muscles. So much for a relaxing swim after a zillion hours on a plane.

'Hello? Is someone there?'

The squeak of the gate and the man's voice had

her grabbing a towel and on alert. And so much for her craved-for peace and quiet. *Go away.* 'Er... hello?'

She switched off the tap, wrapped the towel around her waist and glanced down at her stomach. Well covered. Good. Otherwise whisky-warm-voice man would have a view he'd be unlikely to forget in a hurry.

One glimpse of her scars would leave the poor guy with nightmares. Not as bad as hers, but disturbing enough.

'Hello?' she said again, trying to focus on the blurry image in front of her. She tilted her chin upwards and pretended she was used to entertaining strangers while dressed in four-year-old saggy-bottomed togs and her brother's faded All Blacks towel. 'Can I help you?'

'If you're planning on a swim, forget it,' the tall smudge said. 'I just chucked ten litres of chlorine in.'

'Too late, mate. No wonder my eyeballs feel like melting marshmallows skewered on sharp sticks.' She pointed to her eyes and hoped they didn't look as red as they felt. 'Where I grew up, pool boys left notes if there were excessive chemicals in the pool. It's beyond dangerous. Imagine if a child had jumped in...'

'And where *I* grew up we introduced ourselves before we hurled insults around.' The warmth in his voice vanished, replaced with a tone as cold as the shower water. 'I'm not your damned pool boy. I'm Luke McKenzie.'

The dramatic pause he left hanging in the air made her think she should know that name. The gravitas he projected made her think *everyone* should know that name.

Some NZ idol perhaps? A rugby player? It was lost on her. Two years in the Asian hinterland had her out of step with Kiwi celebrities. 'Yes? And?'

'Your brother's business partner?'

'Ah… Now you come to mention it…' Her cheeks burned as recognition wrestled with embarrassment for prime place in her jet-lag-numbed brain. Big brother Zac had left a note. She'd scanned it as she'd thrown her rucksack down, but hadn't paid much attention.

Luke. The doctor.

Tragic, really. With that frost-tinged dark-velvet voice he was wasted in medicine. 'So you're that Luke.'

'And I assume you're Jessie? You weren't supposed to arrive from Outer Mongolia—or wherever it was you were *finding* yourself—until tomorrow.'

'I was not finding myself. I was working in

Vietnam.' Nice voice, shame about the manners. Typical, but when Zac had begged her to babysit his general practice he'd forgotten to mention she'd be working with Captain Grump. 'I thought I'd get an earlier plane and catch Zac before he headed off. No such luck.'

'He left yesterday. Wanted to get an extra night in Queenstown—the parties are legendary.' The stinging concentrated into a fierce ache behind her eyes. The Blur seemed to get larger. She guessed he'd come closer as a hint of warm citrus and spice male scent hung in the humid air. Very disconcerting. She tried not to inhale.

'Your eyes look hellish. You might need to sloosh them with cold water.'

'You don't say?'

'I do. So you'd better come with me.' Before she could argue, a solid hand steered her into the kitchen and stood her next to the sink.

She shrugged him off. Perfecting the art of keeping her distance from tall, overconfident men had taken a lot of willpower over the last two years. She had no intention of changing that now, melting eyeballs or not. 'Seriously, I'm fine. I can manage.'

'Good job I came back when I did. Chlorine fumes can make you pretty sick. You look cold.'

'Geez, I wonder why.'

He wrapped a towel around her shoulders, apparently oblivious to her shrugging or sarcasm.

In fact, he was surprisingly gentle. Assured and persistent. With a tender touch. Three qualities she'd once admired in a man, then learnt to avoid at all costs. A heady mix experience told her was a recipe for disaster.

Please go. Jessie clutched the towel tightly round her middle, wishing she had something more appropriate to wear. Even though her swimsuit almost covered her from neck to knee, and looked like something Great-Auntie Joan might have worn back in the day, she felt sure her scars were visible. She tried to steal a look but the pain was worse if she moved her eyeballs. 'I've travelled the world on my own. I can manage an eye bath.'

'Stop arguing and tip your head over the basin. I promised Zac I'd look after you.'

'I'm not sure blinding his sister was quite what he had in mind.' Even though her eyes burnt like merry hell she couldn't help responding to the surprise of his laughter. It had a deep quality to it that resounded around the kitchen, absorbing her ill humour. She couldn't stop a giggle as she held her palms up. 'Okay, I'm tipping. I'm tipping.'

'Are you always this melodramatic? I'm only trying to help.' Whereas most men ran a mile from her barbed comments, Luke seemed amused. Why weren't her well-honed distancing techniques working today?

'You'd be more help if you left.'

'Yes, quite the drama queen. Zac didn't warn me about that.'

'How dare…?' Ice water trickled down her face and silenced her retort. It was directed expertly into her eyes and down her hairline. Captain Grump supported her head, stroking her wet hair out of the way, his face only inches from hers. His breath, quickening with every movement, grazed her throat.

Hard muscles brushed against her hip as he curled around her to fill the measuring cup. Warm hands cupped her face as he wiped the water dripping down her chin.

At his touch a weird kind of buzz zinged along her nerve pathways. A buzz that made her want to see his features properly, the colour of his eyes.

Jessie swallowed. *Get a grip.* Since when did eye colour matter? He was an overbearing doctor with little regard for personal space. Although, she conceded, he'd probably see it as dealing with minor trauma.

The last time she was this close to a guy she'd been pumelling Michael's doughy backside with her fists after discovering him having desk sex with the admin assistant. A direct result, he'd insisted, of Jessie's inability to meet his needs.

Looking back, she chose to see the scenario as funny, but she'd learnt the hard way about bombastic doctors with soft hands. So buzzing and zinging were totally off limits.

She shoved both the tacky image of Michael's dimpled bottom and Captain Grump away, then dried her eyes on the towel, grappling for breathing space.

'That's great now. Thanks. You can go.'

'Aw, and I was having so much fun.' His own sarcasm wasn't missed by her. 'I'm going. But if your eyes don't get better, you should get them checked over.'

'You betcha.'

'And if you need anything, just holler.'

'Will do.'

'And Zac asked me to show you around.'

'Another time.' *Like never?*

'Sure.' He sounded relieved. 'We're just across the way, the old white villa.'

Across the way. Great, she'd moved into Wisteria Lane. All nosey neighbours and picture-perfect families. Just what she didn't need. Still, at least that meant he was probably married with a dozen kids—thank the Lord. Someone else to bother with his electric touch and alluring scent.

She'd make sure she wouldn't need anything. 'Absolutely, next time I want my eyes burning out of my skull I'll be right over.'

Through the haze she noted a half-smile.

'Otherwise I'll meet you in the cul de sac, Monday, eight o'clock sharp. I can show you the main sights, bring you up to speed with the practice on the drive to work.' He turned and walked to the door, his long legs covering the distance in no time.

'Hey, wait…' The familiar unease Jessie thought she'd conquered tightened in her stomach. Get in a car with him? Get in a car, period? Her worst nightmare.

Flying, cycling, walking. She could do those, no problem. But driving in an unfamiliar car? Not if she could help it. 'I'd planned to walk. Zac said it's not far.'

'We're always busy Monday morning and I've a lot to tell you. Eight o'clock.' His smile melted and his voice became serious and controlled.

Clearly he was a man used to getting his own way. He stood filling the doorway, one hand resting on the wall. The other hung at his side. Capable hands. Safe. No doubt his driving skills were satisfactory. Surely. Besides, she didn't know the route. Driving would be fine. She shrugged her agreement. Just this once.

Much against her better judgement, Jessie found herself in the cul de sac, clenching and unclenching her fists, Monday morning at eight o'clock. Sharp.

As far as first days went, this was turning into a real doozie. Right up there with the first day of her first period and the first day of double braces.

Damn and double damn.

She glimpsed him on the first-floor decking. 'Hey, Luke. Could I have a quick word before we go?'

He peered down over the neat wisteria-clad balcony. 'Sure. You okay, Jessie?'

'No, I'm not okay. Can you come down here?' Sliding her hands on her hips, she drew herself up to her full five feet three. So not enough. 'This feels like a scene from a Shakespeare play. And you're not pretty enough to be Juliet.'

In what felt like a nano-second he was towering over her. She gulped. Actually—mortifyingly— gulped. Pretty didn't come close. Try devastating.

He looked like he'd stepped out of the pages of a razorblade advert, all proud jaw, taut muscles and tight thighs. Neat and functional dark cropped hair, the complete opposite of her chaotic mop. A pale blue polo shirt and dark grey chinos completed the look of casual professionalism. Every inch the perfect community doctor. Her heart kicked into super-hyper-majorly fast tachycardia.

Her lips dried. Her mouth dried. She spluttered.

Breathe. She found her self-control and pushed it centre stage. No way was she going to be bamboozled by a pretty face. Not again. Dragging a hand across her stomach, she felt the ridged skin and shoved back the memories. Nothing like a gnarly scar to keep a girl centred.

'Don't worry, forget it. We're going to be late.'

'Whoa!' Luke's eyebrows peaked as he so obviously tried to hide a smirk. And failed. 'Man. Your hair.'

'That obvious, huh?' Her heart sank. 'You and your hefty dose of chlorine have turned my hair…'

'Green? This is bad.' *Bad?* Judging by the grin splitting his irritatingly gorgeous chiseled cheeks, this was the most fun he'd had with a locum for a while.

'Go ahead, laugh.'

'Okay, if you insist.'

She nodded as despair toyed with the fading traces of her good humour. She'd so hoped she could do Zac proud. Coming to North Beach had been the first step towards family reconciliation. And she'd been only too pleased to help out, but now look. One step away from utter humiliation.

'Believe me, this is way better than it was. I spent all of yesterday researching cures on the internet and then washing it in different stuff. Tomato paste, baking soda and vinegar. One by one. Over and over.'

Frizz stood out from the sides of her head like unruly garden twine. She tried to smooth it down with her palm. 'If your patients complain about me smelling like a salad dressing, you know why.'

He leaned close and sniffed the top of her head. His soap and shampoo scent had a hint of cinnamon and apple. Freshly laundered cotton strained over broad shoulders as he bent towards her. Shoulders that could take the weight of the world, she imagined, and muscles that were well looked after.

His proximity tormented her fraying nerves and flagging willpower. Her hermitic lifestyle suited her just fine, but sometimes, on very rare occasions, she craved a shoulder to lean against. The comfort of human contact.

And suddenly she had a strange urge to nestle into the crook of his neck—if only she could reach—and breathe every six-feet-too-many-inches of him in. She sighed, hating herself for even thinking of breaking the promises she'd made to herself. Especially with someone so…male.

Was she really that frazzled? It was only a bit of green hair, after all.

'I can't smell anything untoward.' Luke ran a hand over his chin as he regarded her with mock concern. 'Dr Price, I'd like to say your green hair is hardly noticeable but, actually, it is rather loud.'

'If you'd left a note I wouldn't have dived into that pool,' she insisted, laughing despite her misgivings. 'This is all your fault.'

'Sure.' He nodded, his lips curving upwards. 'That's right, blame the helping guy.'

'I'd hate to see what damage you'd do if you were deliberately trying, then.'

'There we go with the melodrama again.' Luke laughed. She was so not what he'd expected. Zac was so laid-back he was horizontal, but his sister was wound as tight as her green-blonde corkscrew hair. Her dark blue eyes had a keep-your-distance glare, and too much sadness for someone so young. She wore a flimsy navy blouse, and snug black pants that clung to those interesting curves he'd glimpsed the other day.

A thumb hooked through her trouser belt loop

and her chin tilted at a defiant angle. Not the most feminine stance, and yet everything about her screamed sensual woman. She was like a fiery pixie, small in stature, big on personality. With a very sharp tongue.

Which, frankly, he could do without. It was taking up way too much of his time. Jessie might turn out to be a damned fine locum, but he couldn't wait until Zac came back and order was restored.

A spark of daring in those dark eyes danced in the dappled early morning light. 'So, do you still want me?'

'What?' He cleared his throat in an attempt to stem a surge of good old male heat. What red-blooded guy wouldn't?

He stepped back. And again. Sure, he'd promised Zac to *be nice* and keep an eye on her, but he needed to force some space. She had an intriguing edgy vulnerability, something he'd learnt to avoid at all costs. 'What kind of question is that?'

'A simple one. I used words of one syllable just to keep it easy for you.' An eyebrow peaked as she pursed her lips. 'You seem a little…distracted. I said, seeing as I look like an advert for swamp chic, do you still want me at the surgery?'

'Oh, I suppose. Zac says you're a very capable doctor. And we are desperate.' She didn't look like she'd be able to lift a scalpel let alone old enough to use one. But somehow, he guessed, she'd know exactly where to stick that blade.

'I ready, Daddy.' Lucy appeared at the front door, clutching her pink rucksack. Luke's heart squeezed. He turned to give his little girl his full attention. 'Hey, sweetheart.'

'Who's dat?'

He picked her up and hugged her close, relishing the feel of his wriggling daughter. Tentatively he was navigating his way through the chaos of solo parenting. The initial gaping hole of disbelief and—at times—outright fear had been filled by a bundle of mischief that demanded his full attention, gave him all of his joy. And most of his stress.

'Have you got your books? Water bottle? Lunchbox?' He ticked off her daily requisites. 'Inhaler? Spare pants?'

Her head bobbed up and down proudly. 'Yes, Daddy. All things.'

'Good girl. That list we made helps, eh?' Would he ever remember everything? Each day, it seemed, her needs changed. She was growing so fast and he was running to catch up.

He breathed in her strawberry anti-tangle shampoo scent and tickled her ribs. She squealed and squirmed as he held on tight. No other female would ever feel this good in his arms.

'Now, this lady is Jessie. She's Uncle Zac's sister and she's going to help me at work.'

'Jessie, this is my daughter.' He turned round to see Jessie's smirk replaced with abject sadness. Tears pricked her eyes. She looked for a second as if her whole world had collapsed.

Then she lifted her chin and tapped her watch. 'Oh. Goodness. Late.'

Deep crimson flushed her cheeks. She flashed a lacklustre half-smile, abruptly stalked to the car and climbed into the passenger seat with no further word.

He followed, irked by her strange reaction. Clipping Lucy safely into her car seat, he bit back a retort. Jessie had obviously been thrown by the sight of his daughter.

But why? Why had she suddenly changed from feisty to flustered?

He slammed the door, unwittingly startling Lucy. Then he blew his daughter a kiss through the window and she wiggled her open palm back. He glanced at the front passenger seat. How was Jessie reacting to that?

No. Stop.

This was exactly the reason women were off

the menu—he didn't have time to waste worrying about what other people thought, whether he'd said or done the wrong thing. He'd learnt pretty rapidly that, where women were concerned, nothing was the right thing. One failed marriage later and he would not be repeating the experience.

So he was not going to grace Jessie's strange actions with a question. The less he got involved with her, the better.

He climbed into the driver's seat, gunned the engine and pulled into the road. 'Everyone okay and ready to go?'

'Fine.' Jessie hung onto the doorhandle and practised her deep-breathing exercises. She could not bring herself to look over her shoulder at the little girl in the back seat. Or at Luke's speedometer. Or at his face. Her hasty retreat to the car had probably appeared rude. Judging by his flattened expression, Luke thought she was a complete fruit loop. She so desperately wanted to get out and walk.

Absolutely the number-one doozie of first days.

Any chance of a rewind? Preferably back to that brief email conversation with Zac where she'd agreed to come and help. Building bridges was all well and good, but there was a limit. Cars and babies were hers. And now she could add green hair to the list.

'You don't look fine.' He glanced at her white knuckles. 'Something wrong?'

'No.'

'First-day nerves?'

'Yeah. Something like that.'

She'd done enough navel-gazing and healing to last a lifetime and was proud of her strength and resilience. So she was surprised at the force of her reaction when she'd seen the little ankle-biter today. Usually she coped well with children, if prepared. It wasn't that she disliked them, far from it. But after her accident she couldn't have them.

Which meant she had to suck up her dreams and get on with her new life. She breathed away the shafts of pain arrowing her solar plexus. Sometimes the brave face she plastered on every day felt a little less brave than she'd like.

Luke slammed his foot on the accelerator and surged onto the highway into speeding traffic. 'Ha! There's often a mini rush-hour at this time. The trick is to nudge in quickly, then we're high and dry.'

'Whoa. Any chance of taking it easy?' Jessie's heart rate notched into hyperdrive as she pumped her foot on an imaginary brake and scanned around for oncoming out-of-control traffic. 'Or has NASCAR shifted to North Beach?'

He shot a glance at her then focused again on the road. 'Sorry. Vietnam's legendary traffic chaos got you spooked?'

'No, I just don't like going fast. It's all good now.' Good now they were travelling in a long line of traffic at no faster than a snail's pace. Yes, tomorrow she'd walk.

'Da-a-addy?' Lucy's voice was more whimper than whine.

'Yes, honey?' Double-chocolate fudge dripped through his response. There was no doubting his affection for his little girl. Love oozed through every word.

'Is Jess the Grinch?'

'No! Lucy!' A sharp intake of breath accompanied his stifled laugh. Jessie could have sworn he blushed. If men did that kind of thing. She was out of practice with what men did, or didn't do. Michael had certainly never blushed. Even when caught with his pants down. She shuddered. Cling onto that image and she'd never look at a man again.

'I'm sorry Jessie, she didn't mean it.' Luke laughed again. 'You're nothing like the Grinch.'

'The what? Okay, tell me, what the heck is a Grinch?'

'It's a...well, it's an evil green creature...' Luke

flicked her a wry smile and shrugged apologetically. Although he didn't look remotely sorry. 'It's a character in a kid's story who tries to steal Christmas. Pretty scary stuff when you're two.'

'Great. So my hair will be giving the children nightmares and the oldies heart attacks!' She pigged her eyes and put on a witchy voice. 'Then my work here will be done.'

'Ah, is that what's eating you? Seriously? The hair? Don't worry.' His smile softened. 'You'll be fine. I'm sure.'

'I wish I could believe you.' Jessie stole a look at his profile. Tiny lines edged his temple. Above the curve of his lip she noticed a diminutive dimple, just small enough to fit the end of her little finger, or the tip of her tongue.

Whoa, that had come out of left field. She pushed it straight back there. Fleetingly something hot shifted in her stomach, like a million butterflies flexing their wings.

Strange. Butterflies? Maybe she did have first-day nerves after all.

From the back of the car Lucy's laughter turned into a cough. A tight whistling wheeze, she noted, on exhalation. A chesty rattle. And again. Then it was gone.

A shadow fell over Luke's face, his features

froze in concern. Just watching his reaction made Jessie's heart slam against her ribcage.

'Lucy? You okay, baby?'

'Okay, Daddy.' She coughed some more.

Jessie twisted to get a glimpse of the toddler and check her pallor. But Luke had clipped her directly behind Jessie's seat. All she managed to see was a pair of chubby legs stuffed into bright red Mary-Janes.

Her heart fluttered and she calmed it. It was just a cough. Lots of kids had them. Why was she thinking of getting involved? The kid's father was a doctor and sitting right there. 'She's probably having a panic attack at sharing a ride with a green-haired Christmas-stealing creature.'

'No. It's fragile asthma.' A frown furrowed his forehead as he glanced at his daughter in the driver's mirror for the tenth time. 'Spent a few nights in hospital over the years. Never want to go there again. The spacer is our friend.' He winked at Lucy. 'Hey, honey? Cough better now?'

'Yes, Daddy.'

'Good girl.' He smiled stiffly as he steered the car into a kowhai-flanked car park in front of a smart colonial-style villa. Yellow flowers glittered in the sunshine. 'It's triggered by stress, excitement, fear—you know, the usual suspects...'

'Scary stuff.' She'd seen too many parents eaten away by worry, watching their child struggle for breath. Luke would be the same. No one could take childhood asthma lightly. 'Maybe you should take some time out with her. Do you want me to check her over?'

'I do the checking.' He jumped out of the car, his expression still closed. He looked across the roof and fixed her with a grey stare. 'She's my daughter, my responsibility. I'll walk her round to crèche, settle her in, then meet you in the staff kitchen. Ten minutes.'

'Oh. Okay. Bye, Lucy.' Jessie blinked at the fast-disappearing pair lost in each other as they walked hand in hand round the corner. Her suggestion of help had brought a weirdly abrupt end to their conversation. Clearly Luke was fiercely protective where his daughter was concerned and didn't welcome any kind of support. Even so, understanding his curt response didn't make it sting any less.

She hauled her bag onto her shoulder and turned to the surgery. That was as far as she would allow her thoughts to go on the matter.

Exhaling deeply, she pushed open the white-painted door and stepped into a sunny reception area. The familiar smell of disinfectant immediately cemented her focus.

This environment was where she felt most at home, behind the mask of her job. Three weeks here, four weeks there, scraping enough to fund her charity work. Helping people. Saving lives. This was her calling, her life.

She slicked a hand over her chaotic curls and breathed in her professional calm. Green hair or not, she was here to do a job, not expend energy on a distraction like Luke McKenzie.

CHAPTER TWO

'A BEE sting? I'll be right there.' Luke shoved away the inconvenient distracting thoughts about his locum that had been flitting in and out of his head all morning, and focused on the emergency. Adrenalin kicked into his gut like a mini-explosion and he relished the buzz it gave him. Managed properly, the outcome would be fine. Managed badly and…

Bee sting. Anaphylaxis. Death.

He hurried down to Reception, to be met by a cacophony and chaos.

A small crowd had formed around a woman who was screaming relentlessly. Her shrieks filled the waiting room, the agony of panic and fear. A flushed child hung from her arms.

'Quick, my boy. Help.' The woman charged at him. 'He can't breathe.'

'Ambulance. Oxygen. Resus trolley,' Luke yelled at his receptionist, ignoring the tearing in his heart at the sight of a desperately sick child. No matter how many times he dealt with this kind of emergency it always threw him back to Lucy in a hospital bed hooked up to a ventilator. But he had no time to surrender to emotion, he needed medical autopilot. 'Room One. Now.'

Grabbing the child, he ran to the closest treatment room, laid the boy on the couch and began to assess.

'Name?'

The boy's mum pushed forward and held her son's hand. Her face was ashen as she struggled to get the words out. 'Ty-Tyler.'

'Age?'

She looked at him, puzzled.

'I need to know for the medicine dosage.'

'Seven.'

'Weight?'

'I don't know…twenty-odd kilos. I think.' Her mouth trembled as her voice wavered again. 'I should know. How could I not know?'

'It's okay. We'll work it out.' Because of Lucy's asthma he knew every single relevant detail of her life, and lots of the irrelevant stuff too. But he couldn't blame this mother. How could she comprehend that knowing a child's weight at any given moment might be important, just in case of an inconceivable emergency?

Tyler's lips had doubled in size, his arms and face and what was visible of his chest in the V of his shirt were covered in angry red hives. His puffed-up eyes screamed out for help as he writhed and clutched his throat. Traces of vomit graced his front. His whole body shook in panic. But he was whimpering. Which meant he could breathe. For now.

Luke checked Tyler's pulse. Rapid and weak. He wrapped an automatic blood-pressure cuff around the boy's arm and waited for its verdict. Dangerously low. Slipping a pulse oxymeter onto Tyler's thumb, he grimaced.

'Come on. Where the hell is that oxygen? The trolley?' Sats dropping, airway almost compromised. Was he supposed to just watch the boy sink into arrest?

This reaction was severe and headed down a perilous path. Anaphylaxis had its own timetable. And it was always too fast.

'Where was he stung?'

'Back of his neck. I put ice on.'

'Any other allergies?'

'No. I should have watched him more closely.' The mother's hands trembled and tears ran down her cheeks. She pulled down the back of Tyler's collar and revealed a livid lump with a tiny black barb sticking out.

Luke grabbed tweezers and yanked the sting out. 'Has he any other medical problems?'

'N-no. Oh, my God. Help him.' She tore at Luke's sleeve, barring his way.

'I'm trying. Please. If you could just wait outside. We need…'

He glanced to the door and beckoned to Maggie, the practice nurse, to take Tyler's mother to a calmer environment. Though he knew every pore of her would strain to stay with her child, his own ghoulish experiences had taught him she would never ever forget the disturbing images that could unfold. He wouldn't wish that on another parent.

As Maggie shuffled the desperate mum away, Luke caught sight of Jessie, portable oxygen tank in one hand and dragging a trolley behind her with the other. Thank God.

Another doctor. Help. That must be why the hairs on the back of his neck had stood to attention at the sight of her. Yes.

Hopefully he wouldn't have to bark orders.

She threw the cylinder onto the bed and switched it on. The reassuring whoosh of pressurised oxygen filled the room. 'Anaphylaxis?'

'Yep. Bee sting. Pretty rapid onset. I need adrenalin. Now.'

'I've got heaps, shame you can't bottle it.' For a millisecond her eyes met his. Her calm dark pupils glistened. Clearly she enjoyed emergency work as much as he did. A shot of heat pumped alongside the adrenalin racing through his veins. He took a steadying breath.

Focus.

As Jessie secured the mask over Tyler's grossly swollen face, Luke snatched out a packet of ampoules and an injection set. He checked the label. 'Adrenaline 1 per 1000. 0.3 mL. Right?' He drew the clear liquid into the syringe and primed the needle. 'Now, I need to get this into him.'

He turned to the child. 'Hold on there, Tyler. Let's get those shorts up, mate. A sharp scratch. Attaboy.'

Luke couldn't wait for more than a nod of consent. 'Stay still. Still.'

If he stopped, just for a second, he could risk this child's life. He dragged up the leg of Tyler's shorts and plunged the life-saving fluid deep into his thigh muscle.

'And I'll secure intravenous access.' Jessie searched the trolley but shook her head. 'Which is the twenty-four gauge? The packaging's different wherever you go.'

'Clear packet.' He directed her to the right-sized luer.

'Got it.' She snapped a tourniquet round Tyler's skinny arm, tapped gently then stabbed the sharp point into his vein. 'Damn, I think his peripherals are shutting down. No, no, wait.'

She peered down, a concentrated frown on her face. The boy's arm flopped to the side as she rubbed and palpated. 'We're good to go. I'll get a line up and some normal saline in.'

The look she flashed him was one of pure relief.

The boy was in shock and needed an urgent boost. If IV access wasn't secured now and his veins shut down completely there'd be hell to pay and a bigger mess when he got to the hospital.

'Well done, Grinch.'

This new look she threw him wasn't so gleeful. But it still had the same effect. A direct hit to his abdomen where it pooled in a shimmering glow. *Damn.* Tyler might be crawling out of the woods but Luke was getting woefully lost in the details of a woman's smile. What on earth was wrong with him today? Find a map and get out quick.

'Mum?' Tyler dragged the mask from his face,

his voice wobbly and weak. His eyes were blood-shot and very, very scared. 'Where's Mum?'

'Steady on, Tyler. I know this sucks.' Luke gently but firmly pushed the mask back over Tyler's face. *Could someone please invent a mask that doesn't frighten the hell out of kids?*

'Doesn't matter if they're disguised as fish, dragons or shaped like kooky lollipops, they still make a scary noise, eh, buddy?' Jessie stroked the boy's head.

Luke stood open-mouthed. 'Are you a mind reader? I was thinking the exact same thing. Weird.'

'What?' She frowned. 'No. It's just scary for them. Keep that there a bit longer, Ty, while the juice works its magic.'

'Want Mum.'

'I'll send someone for her in a minute, mate. Hold still. You're being real brave.' A wriggling patient normally caused Luke a great deal of agro, but this time it meant he'd done his job and saved a life.

Relief surged into his belly. He leaned against the trolley and allowed himself a deep exhalation.

He always worked on autopilot, pushing back any thoughts of what-ifs and maybes, following a path of medical drugs and best practice. The high of his own fight-or-flight chemicals carried him along. But after the event he struggled with the kickback, the jittery blast of emotion and the unassailable desperate truth that one day it might just be his own daughter he was working on.

'Back with us?' Jessie stroked the boy's hair and beamed at Luke. Her eyes lit up, revealing gold flecks in the pools of deep blue. Thick black eyelashes brushed her cheeks and a smattering of freckles crinkled over her nose. Her body relaxed into the smile as she nodded and spoke. 'His resp rate's much better already. Blood pressure rising. Sats at ninety-eight. I can never get over just how quickly adrenalin kicks in.'

'Yeah. They don't call it a *rush* for nothing.'

That smile just about stopped Luke's heart beating. The warmth of it reached right down to his toes, wrapping him in a haze of heat.

But there was more to a woman than a bright smile. Lies, arguments and pain, for example. This was why he spent every day as a single dad. He may be half of an excellent doctoring team, but flying solo at home suited him just fine. It was like a comfortable sofa he'd no intention of updating.

He forced himself to look away and fuss with the luer, finding his equilibrium again.

Tyler's mother's chipped toenails and stripy jandals came into his peripheral vision. He scanned upwards, hoping she hadn't seen the extent to which they'd had to manhandle her child. 'Hi, there. How're you doing?'

'Is he okay? What happened?' Her voice trembled.

Luke wrapped an arm round her, helped her find a spot to sit next to her son. He knew how much she'd be wanting to touch Tyler, hold him, breathe him in. 'It's okay. He's going to be fine. Yes, you can hold his hand. He's a bit of a pin cushion, though and he's been through the wars.'

He rubbed his knuckles across the boy's head and ruffled his hair. The kid smiled weakly and Luke felt a comradely connection. 'I reckon he deserves a treat later. Maybe when he gets the all-clear, ice cream might be nice?'

Jessie watched in awe. Forget bombastic. Commanding. Empathetic. Luke's velvet voice had taken on a lulling tone, so calming. *Trust me*, it said.

It certainly seemed to be working on Tyler and his mum, who gazed at him, solemn as he reassured them.

He did everything by the book. Assessing, acting, anticipating. And all with genuine compassion.

'As you know, Tyler had an allergic reaction to a bee sting.' Luke held the woman's hand and now focused entirely on her as he spoke. 'We've given him an injection to help, but sometimes the reaction can come back. So we'll keep an eye on him in hospital for a day or so. Has this ever happened before?'

'No. Never. It was horrible.' She shivered and turned to Jessie. 'You saved his life. Thank you.'

'Hey, really, it's my job. He might have to carry a special injection around with him after this. Just in case he gets another sting, and another reaction this bad.'

Jessie twisted to check on their patient. She'd been holding his wrist and monitoring his pulse. 'He's getting a better colour in his lips now. His heart's still racing, but that'll be from the bolus of adrenalin. It saved his life, but it can give a heck of a kick to the system.'

Maggie popped back into the room and glanced at each of them in turn. 'Oh, good. Ambulance is here. I'll show them in.'

After twenty minutes and a detailed handover Jessie stood in Reception and watched Luke say goodbye to his patient. A buzz of excitement still thrilled round her body. Excess adrenalin was always hard to shake off. At least, she put it down to the medical emergency and not the view.

Luke had handled everything with a professionalism and calm that had had everyone doing his bidding. And yet she'd never seen a more compassionate and composed doctor. His morning clinic had ended with a bang and he still remained as fresh as if the day had just begun. Still Dr Perfect. How did he manage it?

Unlike her. She ran a hand over her hair and looked round for a mirror. Scarecrow chic now probably.

Alarm bells rang loudly in her head. Since coming back to New Zealand, she'd become more and more concerned about how she looked. What did it matter all of a sudden? Appearances didn't matter. Work did. Saving lives did. Tyler did.

Of course, it was easy—scratch that, *essential*—for a woman with scars to believe that. Anything else would be just plain stupid. Or egotistical suicide. And she certainly wasn't into that.

Luke's eyebrows rose as he closed the front door and turned to her. 'Thanks for your help in there. You're one hell of a doctor.'

Heat shunted up her neck. Yes, she was a good doctor. But it felt great hearing it from a colleague. 'Ditto. Are you okay?'

'Sure. Why not?'

'I just thought, having Lucy, it must be hard dealing with sick littlies.' She knew how hard it was and was giving him a let-out to voice it. 'We don't just have to suck it up, you know. It can be good to talk about it.'

'I'm fine. Seriously.' His back straightened and his shoulders pushed back. If he had any kind of fatherly concerns, he wasn't going to share them. 'We handled everything by the book, I'd say.'

And so she left it. There was a faint question in his eye, then a shut-down look like the one in the car. He clearly wasn't comfortable talking about his life or Lucy or his worries.

She shrugged and changed the subject. 'Turning into an interesting first day.'

'You can say that again.'

He stopped in front of her, jotted a note, signed some prescriptions. As he wrote, fluidly and neatly for a doctor, his shoulders relaxed and his features softened. Then he turned to her and smiled. His blue-grey eyes were like burnished steel, sparked with a heat that reached to her belly. 'I would like to invite you to lunch.'

'Oh?' No need for the hackles. The guy was probably married. Although he wore no wedding band. No white mark. No mention of a wife. Good grief, how did she know that?

'I usually do a quick debrief at the sushi bar on a locum's first day. But unfortunately I have a load of errands to run. It's Lucy's birthday next week and I'm on party duty. Maybe later in the week?'

She breathed out deeply. 'No worries, I'll grab a roll and catch up on paperwork. Maybe familiarise myself again with the resus trolley.'

She flashed him a conspiratorial smile. Memorising the colour-coded packs on the resus trolley was a matter of professional pride. Besides, hours out of his presence would be a fine idea. Then perhaps she could work out why she'd made a study of his left ring finger. 'Hope you get it all sorted.'

'Petting zoos and bouncy castles? I doubt it. There's way too much to get my head around. And I thought medical finals were hard.' He turned. 'Maybe we can debrief later? After surgery. Five o'clock.'

'I was hoping to get home…'

But he was gone.

'Okay, see you later.' Jess sighed. So, he lived a busy life. Full-time doctor and very hands on dad. Hopefully tonight's meeting would be quick if he had a family to go home to and a party to arrange.

She looked round the empty reception area and pushed him out of her head. Where to start? Resus trolley? Sushi?

But that made her think of him again.

'Oh.' He stuck his head back around the door, making her jump almost out of her skin. 'Daft idea, but I don't suppose you know anything about organising parties for a three-year-old? To be honest, I'm flummoxed by it all. I'm told fancy dress is mandatory. Apparently.'

'Er...no.' Typical, he'd come back just as she'd been able to breathe normally again and now her breath had been snatched away. She couldn't remember the last party she'd been to, kid's or otherwise. Invites weren't exactly forthcoming when she moved around enough not to forge any meaningful relationships.

She pressed against the reception desk, grateful to lean against something solid. Almost instinctively her palm ran over the hard knobbles and knots of skin over her abdomen. She cradled the emptiness, the place where she'd once felt her baby kick. Now a mess of scarred tissue. A shaft of pain exploded in her stomach. She breathed it away, shook her head. No. No kid's parties. And no point dwelling on the past.

'Sorry. No idea. I'm definitely the wrong person to ask.'

'Ah, well, worth trying.'

Dragging on a smile, she shrugged. 'Anyway, shouldn't you be discussing parties with Lucy's mum?'

'Yeah, right.' His jaw muscles tightened as he turned back towards the corridor. 'Forget it, I'll sort it out.'

Brilliant. Deep joy. Talk about putting her two size sevens straight into her big, stupid, careless mouth.

Jessie stared at the computer screen, trying to concentrate on the next patient's notes. But so many new questions crowded her head. Why wouldn't Luke talk to Lucy's mother about organising parties? The only clues she had were the flicker of disdain in his eyes and the clenched cheek muscle; clearly relations between him and the girl's mother were strained.

'Excuse me? Jessie?' Maggie bustled into the room, dragging Jessie away from her reverie. 'Any chance you can see Kyle Phillips soon? He's tearing around the waiting room and driving his mum close to tears.'

'Of course. I was just about to call him in.'

'I could ask Luke to squeeze him in if you're too busy.' Maggie looked pointedly around the empty room, no doubt wondering why on earth they'd employed such a slacker. 'He usually sees Kyle, but he's double-booked most of this afternoon. Shame, they've just pitched up on the off chance we could fit them in.'

Jessie's stomach tumbled at the mention of Luke's name. Traitorous stomach, it was way more interested in him and his business than was good for her.

But her head wasn't. Michael had sealed her belief that relationships and her couldn't work. Discovering her husband's infidelity after her accident, losing her baby and then her marriage, had tattooed a promise onto her heart. *Never again.*

'Yes, yes, of course, send Kyle in right away.' *And stop me thinking about Luke and his smile.*

Was she thinking about his smile now too? What the hell happened to *never again*? So he had a cute smile. Perfect teeth. Big deal. Probably paid a zillion dollars in dentistry.

Despite the urgency to get the next patient in, Maggie seemed to prefer talking about her employer. 'Luke's always so punctual, his clinics never run late. Don't know how he manages it, what with little Lucy. She's a handful. But he has everything organised to work around her routine.'

'Sounds like he's a regular miracle worker.'

'It was a big shock, you know, and such a change for him. He hadn't a care in the world a few years ago—a big social life, partying.'

'Partying?'

'As soon as he had Lucy he put all that behind him. He's doing so well as a solo parent.'

Aha. Now the fog lifted. 'Sounds like I'll be hearing lots more about him over the next few weeks.' Hopefully like what the heck had happened to Lucy's mother and how come Luke managed not to have a care in the world when he had a family to provide for?

Jessie looked at the computer clock.

'I'm five minutes late already.' She slid her chair back and tried to look like she meant business. 'I'd better catch up.'

Stacey Phillips shifted in her seat and placed a trembling hand on her three-year-old's shoulder. 'For goodness sake, sit still, Kyle, and let the doctor look in your ears.'

'It's okay, Mr Wriggle-Bottom, I've finished looking now.' Jessie replaced the auroscope on its charger and smiled at Kyle's mum. 'Your instincts were right. Kyle has a slight redness on his eardrum, caused by a viral infection, but it's nothing serious. Antibiotics won't be any use because they attack bacteria, not viruses, but paracetamol will help with the pain. Bring him back if things don't settle down.' Jessie ruffled the boy's blond locks, handed him a toy train. 'Here, Kyle, show Mummy the train while I write in your notes. Choo-choo.'

'Ahh….choooooo.' Kyle sneezed, all over Jessie's trousers. *Great.* A snot-coloured sticky patch to match her snot-coloured hair. She bit her lip and held in a smile. Her locum pay had better include laundry bills.

The young mother's face crumpled, her eyes red-rimmed and brimming with tears. 'I'm so sorry. Really sorry. Kyle, say sorry to the doctor. Naughty boy. Naughty.'

It seemed an extreme reaction to a sneeze. Maybe she was just the anxious type.

'It's fine, Stacey. They'll wash. Worse things happen, believe me. He couldn't help it.' Jessie pointed to her shoulder. 'Sticky patch number one, vomit from a two-year-old. There's felt tip on my sleeve from an uncoordinated six-year-old. I've got four more hours of clinic to get completely covered in gloop. Things are just warming up.'

Stacey seemed appeased by this, but her twitchy demeanour and puffy red face gave Jessie cause for concern. She leaned forward and touched her hand. 'Is there anything else?'

Stacey shook her head, reached for a tissue, wiped her eyes and the boy's nose. 'We should go, I suppose, you're busy.'

But instead of standing up, Stacey stayed where she was, tears refilling her eyes. As she wrung her hands in her lap, her knee jerked up and down apace. 'Kyle, please for once sit still.'

Ignoring the flashing on her computer announcing that her next client had arrived, Jessie waited. Stacey needed time and space. Phooey to Luke, Patron Saint of Perfectly Run Clinics. Sometimes patients needed extra attention. 'Are you worried about something, Stacey?'

Stacey's hand hovered over her mouth as if holding her words in. She bit her lip and looked away. 'I missed a period.'

'You think you might be pregnant?' Jessie lowered her voice to prevent Kyle hearing.

'Yes. I have sore boobs and I feel sick pretty much all of the time.' Stacey's chin quivered. 'Just like last time.'

'And you're not happy about it?'

'No. My husband's just left me. I can't cope with two kiddies on my own.' She looked over at her three-year-old now sitting on the floor engrossed in *The Monster Book of Dragons*. 'I can't cope with one. I don't think I want this.'

'I understand.' Jessie nodded and a lump wedged under her diaphragm, pressing deep, catching her breath. Dealing with pregnant mums always brought back an echo of the sadness that had lingered in her bones far too long.

It was the small details that had surprised her the most; how, in the pregnancy books, foetal development was measured in terms of fruit. The size of a strawberry, then a lime, then a grapefruit. She used to joke about how she was going to give birth to a fruit salad.

And how being pregnant had been like carrying the happiest secret ever. And that as her belly had swelled so had her heart. Chock full of love for someone she'd never even met.

She squashed the swell of emotions rising in her chest. Now was not the time to remember these things. She would never let her own experiences interfere with her practice. Stacey needed a coherent, competent doctor not a gloomy one.

'The thing is, I wanted a baby, my husband didn't.' Stacey's lip wobbled. 'I thought I could convince him, but all we did was argue.'

'Sometimes life gets hard, Stacey. I know. Truly.'

Stacey ripped a tissue into fragments and let them drop onto her lap like a tiny snowdrift. 'I can't have a baby. It's not the right time. I don't know what I'm going to do.'

'Whatever happens, you'll get through this. Trust me.' It did get easier, she knew that from painful experience. It was amazing what you could survive.

Jessie picked up the tissue scraps and put them in the bin, then took hold of Stacey's hand. 'Let's not jump ahead of ourselves. First, I'll get Maggie to do a pregnancy test.'

'Oh, no.' The colour drained from Stacey's blotchy face. 'Not Maggie. She's my husband's aunt and word spreads so fast here. North Beach is a small town. Small minds make big gossip, my mum used to say. I don't want him knowing. Not yet. Not until I've got my head around it. Please don't tell anyone.'

'Of course not, although I will have to write something in your notes. But seeing as this is Kyle's consult, I can't think why anyone would need to look at your information. Rest assured, Stacey, I'm here to help. And I won't tell a soul.'

Luke regarded the view of the swamp pixie's taut derrière as she stretched to the back of the drug cupboard, and tried to ignore the fizz of heat in his abdomen.

What the heck was going on with his body these days?

He almost groaned in frustration. Weird. He

couldn't remember his hormones ever being this out of sync with his brain.

He battled against this unfamiliar surge of lust. Yes, she was hot. But there were plenty of hot women around.

It felt like over the last two years every emotion had been caught in a weird freeze-frame and now someone—*Jessie*—had flicked a switch on his awareness scale. And it had spiked.

Inconvenient. And temporary, he'd make sure of that. Dragging back the memory of her odd behaviour that morning, he attempted to activate his 'off' switch. As he glanced at her butt again the switch refused to budge.

Damned irritating. All his knowledge of Jessie so far suggested she was a typical, selfish drifter type. Just like Chloe. Endlessly appealing and ethereal. Promising everything and giving nothing. Oh, except a baby to look after.

Professional courtesy deemed he remove his eyes from Jessie's backside and make polite conversation. 'How's it going? Got over this morning's drama?'

Jessie twisted and peered up at him. The tight corkscrew hair had softened and tendrils framed her face, giving an almost angelic impression. Apart from an odd milky smudge on her shoulder and a large stain on her knee. And the far from angelic stare.

The pulse at her slender throat beat a rapid tattoo and it took a mammoth effort not to place his hand on it, count the beats, touch her skin. But he managed it.

An eyebrow rose as she spoke. 'Um. What? Sorry?'

'Ah, nothing. Forget it.'

'Forgotten already.' She turned her back to the cupboard and fumbled in her pocket. Then quickly walked away. Was it his imagination, or were her cheeks red?

He watched Jessie's quickened pace down the corridor. Her delicate way-too-grown-up blouse pulled across a taut ridge of shoulder muscle, and her clenched fists, the jerky movement of her hand to her pocket all sounded alarm bells in his head.

She didn't look flustered, she looked hunted. He'd seen that look on a woman's face before— when he'd discovered Chloe's one-way plane ticket out of North Beach. Her get-out-of-jail-free card, she'd called it. Free? He'd unwittingly footed the bill when she'd *borrowed* his credit card.

Still, hunted was not at all how he expected a locum to act. Something in her manner didn't add up. 'Did you find what you were looking for, Jess?'

She slowed, but didn't stop. Her hand curled next to her trouser pocket. 'It's Jessie. Or Jessica. No one calls me Jess. I don't like it. I'm. Fine.'

'You sure?'

Swivelling on her heel, she pierced him with dark blue eyes, the flush of her cheeks now a rash down her neck. A frown etched deep across her forehead. 'Luke, I'm busy.'

He glanced at her slim fingers as they stole into her pocket. She was hiding something. His pulse jittered.

Keep calm. It may just be nothing. 'You've just seen Kyle Phillips, haven't you?'

'Yes.'

'Everything okay? Didn't need anything for him?'

'No.' She threw him a tight smile and tapped her watch. 'Got to go. Don't want to upset the time police.'

As she turned she stumbled against the wall. 'Stupid heels.'

A packet fell from her pocket to the floor as she edged down the corridor.

'Hey, you dropped something.'

'Oh.' It was more a sigh than a word. She bent to the floor at the same time as he did.

His hand covered the packet.

Her hand covered his and her heat infused his skin. His gaze shot to her face. Wide blue eyes stared up at him. Her teeth bit into her bottom lip.

She shook her head, a tiny movement that shouted, *Don't ask*.

He didn't. He couldn't. Words lost their way from his brain to his mouth.

God, she was lovely. An ache stole into his stomach. His heart pounded. His lips dried.

Whatever the heck she'd been doing, whatever she'd been hiding, he didn't care.

Suddenly he wanted to feel the bow of her lips against his, press against her curves, let her body tell him the answers to all those questions zinging around his head.

What? Kiss her? Here? In full view of his staff?

Since when did lust place before trust?

Lust. For God's sake, where did this sudden weakness come from? Women like Jessie were poison, and he sure as hell wasn't tempted to have a shot.

Plus, he was in the middle of the double-booked clinic from hell, with no time to analyse this self-destructive reaction to a locum. He just needed to gain some self-control.

'I've got it.' He snatched his hand from under hers, dragging his gaze away from those captivating eyes, and unfurled the packet from his fist. 'There you are. Oh, a pregnancy test. Is that all?'

Even the tops of her ears were red as she grabbed the packet and straightened her blouse down over her hips. 'Thanks.'

'All this fuss over nothing.' He blew out a long breath. He had totally misread the situation. Letting memories of Chloe get in the way of a decent working relationship. 'Maggie usually sorts the tests out, I'll give her a shout. Tell the patient to wait in the nurses' area.'

'It's…. No. I can handle it.' Her eyes flicked towards the bathroom. 'I'll do it myself.'

Luke's stomach plummeted a thousand feet.

Fool.

Three-year-old Kyle Phillips certainly didn't need a pregnancy test. Jessie's next patient was Frank Carrington, so unless the IVF schedule had been extended to eighty-year-old kumara farmers, the pregnancy test must be hers.

'Sorry. I didn't mean to pry.'

Head cocked to one side, her mouth slanted then curved into an O shape. She waved the packet in the air.

'You thought this was for me?'

Her eyes darkened as she, almost subconsciously, it seemed, ran a hand across her belly. He'd seen her do that a few times—in the car, when she'd first seen Lucy and again now. Unusual. Some kind of nervous reflexive reaction. Like nail biting or toe tapping.

A bitter-sweet laugh erupted from her lips as she walked back into her consulting room. 'I don't think so, Luke. Now, I really do have to get on.'

'Of course.' He stared at the space she'd left and rubbed a hand over the back of his neck, shaken by his visceral reaction to her. Boy, oh, boy, he'd need therapy by the time this woman had finished her three-week stint.

Once he'd have tried to work her out, enjoyed the thrill of the chase, just for the hell of it. But things had got complicated and he'd been badly burnt.

Jessie's private life was none of his business, and it would stay exactly like that until she left.

CHAPTER THREE

AFTER a long day, an overrun clinic and a debrief, all Jessie wanted was to go home and fall asleep. A gentle stroll back seemed perfect on such a balmy summer's evening, work off a few pounds and sort through these disconcerting thoughts she was having about Luke. Exercise and exorcise—the perfect double whammy.

She wandered out to the parking lot to get her bearings.

'Jess? Thought you'd left already. Need a ride? Or are you happy to walk?' Luke strode across the shimmering tarmac, an easy nonchalance rippling through his step.

Damn. Just when she thought she could relax.

Better be polite. He probably already thought she was a paid-up member of the fruit-loop clan. 'No, thank you, walking's good.'

'No worries.' He leaned against the door of his station wagon, laughter lines edging his tired eyes. 'I guess that was probably a baptism by fire?'

'For some reason, I thought sleepy North Beach would be a breeze. But it's nothing I can't cope with.'

'I don't doubt it, Dr Price. Having seen you in action, I reckon you could handle just about anything.'

The slate-blue of his irises intensified in the evening sunlight as he fixed Jessie with his gaze. A smile fluttered over his lips.

Lips she suddenly had an urge to press her mouth against.

Good Lord. Where had that come from? That wouldn't go down so well on her first day. It was so inappropriate it was almost funny. But the sudden heat in her abdomen wasn't.

Wow. *No. Impossible.* Men hurt. And she wasn't a masochist. She needed to go home right now.

'The question is, Jessie, are you coming back tomorrow?'

'Only if you pay for the dry cleaning.'

She pointed to the gloop patches. Noting with irritation that she was unwittingly drawing attention to her body. He obligingly scanned down her body. A hot tingling prickled from the top of her head to the soles of her feet.

No. She'd never tingled before. With Michael it had been homey and comfortable, not out of control. At least until he'd snatched all control away by sleeping with their employee. This was just a post-work chat between colleagues. Nothing more.

She shrugged, trying to control her ragged breathing. 'Occupational hazard, I guess.'

'That's kids for you,' he agreed, drawing her gaze back to his face, his sharp cheekbones, that perfect mouth of his. She had to concentrate on his words, not on the way his lips moved so sensually. Or the way her mouth suddenly felt so parched.

She ran a tongue over her bottom lip and saw a shot of awareness in his eyes as he spoke. 'I bet I can identify each of those stains from fifty paces.'

'That's some strange kind of skill. But whatever works for you.'

'I'm a man of many talents.' His eyebrows peaked suggestively.

'And *I* don't doubt that, Dr McKenzie.'

A fist of desire wedged into her abdomen as she imagined the many talents of his mouth, his hands and what magic they could do to her.

She looked away and focused on dampening down the heat in her face. She knew all about men's magic, their tricks and deceit. Luckily she also knew enough tricks to put up a barrier—like keeping the conversation along uncontroversial non-sexual lines until she could politely escape to the safety of her own home.

'Er…you mentioned Lucy's mum earlier? Maggie said…'

'Maggie's always saying something. Don't pay any attention. She means well, I guess.' His face became serious. He looked at his watch, then slammed the door on that topic of conversation. 'Look, Zac asked me to show you around. I have five minutes. You want to take a look at the beach?'

Did she? 'Don't put yourself out on my account. I can do my own sightseeing.'

'I'm sure your brother would have a heap of things to say about that. It's pretty special down there. You'll regret it if you don't take a look. And I'll get an ear bashing.'

'I'm sure you'll cope.' Those broad shoulders looked like they'd cope with anything life threw at him.

His eyes glinted as he flashed a devil-may-care smile. He glanced at his watch again. 'Take it or leave it. But hurry up and decide. Five minutes, Jessie. That's all I'm offering.'

'Then that's all I'll take.' She could spare five minutes to share Zac's favourite place. Five minutes. Then three short weeks. And after that normal life would be resumed. Away from North Beach and Luke irritatingly alluring McKenzie.

She tried to keep up with him down the path, past fenced-off sand dunes and through brown grasses that tickled her ankles. She slipped off her heels and relished the feeling of hot, gritty sand between her toes. A gentle offshore breeze licked her skin, delightfully refreshing in the sticky evening heat.

His citrus scent wafted towards her, forcing memories of their encounter over her sink. She hung back, creating a gulf of space between them, regretting agreeing to something so unwise.

While the shivers of desire were delicious and unfamiliar, they shoved out her common sense and ushered in danger. Five minutes of sightseeing, then she'd make her excuses and leave. Pronto.

Luke stopped by a cluster of volcanic silver-black rocks hewn into a ragged bench. Rays of sun glinted off them, making them sparkle like gems. 'Sometimes I come here to shrug off work before I go home.'

'Seriously, shouldn't you be going back? What about Lucy?'

'She'll be fine. Her childminder picks her up from crèche.'

'Sounds like you have a busy life.'

'No different to any other single parent.' He faced her, suddenly serious. 'Lots of people have it worse than me.'

Although he hadn't always thought that.

Jessie looked at him like she needed an explanation. He was shocked at his willingness to share details about his private life. But Zac or Maggie would no doubt fill her in anyway. She may as well get it from the horse's mouth. No frills or gossip, no opinion or conjecture. 'Lucy's mum ran out on us.'

'Oh.' Jessie's face fell. Clearly she hadn't been expecting something so…unconventional. Men left. Women…mothers…stayed. Usually.

'You don't have to tell me, really.'

'It's no secret. It's a big grapevine, you'll hear eventually.'

He kicked his foot into the sand, watched the tiny grains slide off his shoe and tried to stem the rising bitterness, ease the pain in his chest. He'd tried to make his marriage work. Failing had been hard. Enough to put him off trying again. 'I'm not proud to say Lucy is the product of a brief holiday romance.'

'Maggie said you liked to party.'

'Yeah, me and Zac had quite a reputation in the old days.'

He held in a smile as he remembered the scrapes

they'd found themselves in. Only having a daughter had been the biggest and the most intense. And the final nail in the coffin of wild, wicked days.

'Lucy's mum, Chloe, was just passing through between festivals. I knew her less than a week and waved her on her way. Imagine my surprise when she turned up nine months later about to pop.'

'Oops.' Jess's eyes widened and she gave him a sympathetic smile. But she didn't have that judgmental look that most people wore when they discovered his playboy error. 'That must have been hard for you.'

'Yeah. Lucy was a big mistake. I tried to do the right thing, married Chloe quickly, but she just couldn't handle this kind of life. One night she left me, literally, holding the baby.'

'How old was Lucy when Chloe left?'

'Eight months. She'd just got to the separation anxiety stage. Hell on earth, believe me.'

He smiled a little. 'I can laugh about it now. But back then it was crazy. Juggling work and sleepless nights with a screaming baby. Utter chaos.' And yet being a father was the most amazing, scary thing that had ever happened to him. 'Poor kid, she didn't understand. One day her mother was here, the next she was gone.'

Jess sat down next to him on a rock. Her hands twisted in her lap. Her knuckles were white and her cheeks an angry red. 'Chloe must have had a strong reason to walk away from her child. I can't imagine what drives a mother to do that.'

'Beats me. She was young, *not meant to be tied down*, she said. Hated order and any kind of routine.' He shrugged and rubbed his chin, quelling the acrimony he'd thought he'd overcome. He *had* overcome. It had taken a lot of work. Raising a baby had been an overwhelming distraction. 'She hated everything I'd created for her—the suburban house, the regular lifestyle. She went off to *find* herself.'

'Seems to me she lost everything,' Jess murmured.

For some reason this story seemed to be affecting his new locum deeply. She looked up at him with soulful eyes and he had an inexplicable urge to wrap his arms around her.

No. He stopped himself. That kind of reaction would be reckless in the extreme. And he didn't do reckless, not any more. Especially not in the middle of a conversation about his ex-wife. She was a cautionary tale in herself.

'I'm so sorry, Luke,' Jess said sincerely.

'Hey, don't be. I'm over it. I'm the lucky one, I have Lucy.' And determination to keep away from drifters, women and relationships altogether.

'Do you think Chloe will ever want this life back?' she asked.

'Who knows? She signed all care over to me and has only been in touch once to talk about a divorce and demand a pay-off. She didn't even ask about Lucy. But she has rights, and I would never stop her visiting her child.'

And he'd deal with that if and when it happened. 'Right now I'm trying to be a father and mother. I still can't get the hang of the technical stuff, like braids and tights, and I panic at the thought of puberty.' Meanwhile, the stash of parenting books by the side of his bed grew exponentially.

'I only saw you two together for a few minutes, but Lucy clearly adores you. You're a good doctor, if that's anything to go by. Zac likes you. And you seem to have your head screwed on okay, for a bloke. You'll be fine.'

'I hope so.' Maybe she was right. But, then, she hardly knew him.

Jessie understood that talking about this was a big deal for Luke. However much he didn't want to admit it, he'd been hurt. No wonder he micro-managed his life and his time, making order out of chaos.

He'd lost a lot. A spouse, trust. God knew, Jessie understood how that felt. But at least he'd man-aged to keep the one thing that would elude her for ever. A child. *His child.* In having that much, he was the luckiest person alive.

Her heart constricted at their kindred experi-ences but she clamped down on a sudden impulse to wind her hand into his tight fist. She'd do it with a patient, empathise. But giving in to temp-tation to touch Luke could only lead to disaster. Been there, done that, got the scars to prove it. Inside and out.

She put on her happy face and remembered all the things she had to be grateful for. Health and independence counted for a lot these days.

After two years she'd managed to keep a lid on everything, and even though it felt like her core had been stirred up in the last two days, she was going to screw that lid back on tightly.

Picking up a pebble, Luke skimmed it across the sparkling water. One bounce. Two. Three…

'Three? Is that all? Bet I can beat that.' Jessie laughed, jumped up, found a flat, smooth stone and sent it gliding across the top of the waves. 'Four, five, six!'

'Wow!' He turned to her, the heat in his eyes dazzling. His dark mood had passed. 'Impressive.'

She grinned triumphantly. Where most kids grew up with technology to amuse them, she'd had books and rocks and dirt to occupy her time. Life out in the geological field was dull in the extreme. But at least it wasn't wasted. 'I like to think I've mastered most of the important life skills. You should see me with a catapult.'

'Is there anything you can't do?'

'Lots and lots.'

Like have children. Happy families? She bent to choose another rock, all the better to hide her red face. Maybe one day she'd find the courage to tell him her story. But right now she'd had enough of pity parties.

He picked up a stone. 'Okay. This time I'll match you. Six?'

'Yeah? Go on. I'd like to see you try.' Jessie watched the stone skim above the translucent waves, bouncing and curving. The flex of his broad shoulders as he stretched made her want to run her fingers over them. Why was she finding everything about him so appealing?

'Five. Six! Yes!' He gave her a superhero pose, his biceps twitching impressively. 'I am brilliant.'

'Well,' she said dryly, 'everyone at work seems to think the sun shines out of your...'

She squinted closely at his taut backside, then over his shoulder at the sun melting into the horizon in a haze of red and orange. 'Oh, no, it's over there. Wow, what a gorgeous sunset. What an amazing place.'

Luke didn't turn to look, didn't follow her raised hand pointing out to the ocean, didn't move his eyes away from her face. 'Yes. It's a great view all right.'

His intense expression burned into her, a yearning, a longing—for her? And her body responded as if on autopilot. Every fibre ached to touch him. No matter how hard she fought it, this attraction seemed to have a will of its own.

Not knowing what to do or where to look, she turned and walked along the water's edge. The cool sea lapped at her ankles as she swished through the foamy shallows.

He caught her up. But stayed a few feet away. The tension simmered between them like static. Every part of her trembled in anticipation of his touch. She wanted to curl into him, press her body against his, feel the vibrancy of him.

She thought about brushing her arm against his, just to bring about some relief.

But that would be so stupid. Stupid with a capital S.

'Jess? You okay?' His voice was like melting dark chocolate. Thick and rich and inviting, pouring through her.

'Just thinking about this place,' she lied, grasping for a distraction from him.

Even from this distance she felt his body relax, heard his breathing slow.

'So you never visited North Beach before?'

'No. I wanted to, but things never seemed to work out.'

'Zac said he hadn't seen you for a while.'

Regret whipped through her. The shame of putting off a visit for so long. But it had seemed easier that way. Years of no contact with her family had left a hole she was now trying to fill. It was just typical that Zac wasn't around to see her try. But, then, she'd probably hurt him most with her silence.

'I can see why he settled here, it's so peaceful,' she said.

'It took him a while. He said he was allergic to putting down roots. Guess that runs in the family? But North Beach got under his skin. He reckons

it's just far enough from the city to feel perma-
nently on holiday, and soothingly beautiful for
hangovers.'

He smiled ruefully. 'Plus, after a spectacularly
hedonistic night out he signed my contract and
can't afford to buy out of it.'

'You got my brother drunk and made him sign
his life away?' She batted him on his shoulder.

He playfully jumped away onto the firm sand.
'Zac managed to do that all by himself. And I
think the decent salary and flexible hours to work
with his beloved Auckland Panthers helps.'

She edged out of the water and flicked the drips
off her feet. 'I should have known it had more to
do with rugby than with settling down.'

'I think he's finally enjoying a regular income
and a regular job. You should try it.'

'Not likely.' She shook her head, surprised at the
tinge of jealousy she felt over her brother's appar-
ent nesting instincts kicking in. It certainly wasn't
something they'd been nurtured with growing up.
Not that they'd been nurtured with anything much.
'I like to keep moving. Six weeks in Dunedin after
this, then who knows?'

'You seriously enjoy living like that? Drifting?'

No. Yes. No. She didn't know any more. 'I've

spent the whole of my life on the road, can't seem to stop.'

Not strictly true; she had stopped once. But it would be literally impossible to do it again. Losing her baby, her fertility and her husband in one nightmare month had made her crave her nomadic lifestyle again. Losing herself in anonymity had saved her.

'I reckon Zac would like you to stick around for a while.'

Me too, his expression said. Or did she just imagine that? Impossible indeed. But the thought simultaneously thrilled and frightened her. They came from different places, had very different dreams.

'I have a contract in Dunedin starting the day before Zac gets back here. So I'm going to miss him,' she admitted, swallowing her disappointment.

The rhythmic calm of the waves lulled her into silence.

Seagulls and terns hopped along the shoreline, screeching and fighting for scraps in the flotsam. A tiny triangle of white bobbed on the glittering water, a fishing boat trawling for today's catch. The place radiated peace. Something that had eluded her for a long time. That she'd finally achieved.

And which vanished every time she set eyes on

Luke McKenzie. She chanced another look at him, at his serious profile and that perfect mouth.

Maybe if she kissed him, felt his heat on her, just once. Expunged this crazy hunger for him. Just got it out of her system. Maybe she'd find that peace again.

Panic exploded in her chest. Had she really just thought that? Give in to passing lust and break all her promises? Put her neck out on that fragile line? No way. Crazy was the best way to describe it.

He laughed. 'You like moving, and I like staying put.'

'Funny.' She swallowed hard, awareness flaring through her. Was he thinking the same thing? That opposites attracted? Nonsense. They couldn't take this anywhere.

Beside her, Luke's breathing quickened as he turned to her. 'Jessie…'

'Yes, Luke?' She looked up at him with questions and promises firing in her eyes. Her moist lips parted ever so slightly, tempting him to break every resolution he'd made.

Years ago he'd have thought nothing of kissing a woman and forgetting all about it. He couldn't do that now, not with Lucy to consider. Not with the memory of Chloe burning a hole in his head.

He knew everything there was to know about

being left high and dry by women driven by self-interest. He could write the manual on it.

But there was something about Jessie. Her feisty, smart mouth and hidden vulnerability that made him want to protect her. And the fact she was as sexy as sin.

His heart pounded fast and furious in his chest as she raised her hand towards his chest.

He touched her fingers, and her skin felt cool and soft. He hated himself as he did it. He'd meant to pull her hand away, but somehow he hadn't been able to.

This was mad. He was seriously out of control.

'I don't think we should…' Words got lost somewhere between his head and his mouth. Her fingertips seared the tiny hairs on his skin. Heat from her body stoked the burning that flooded through him. He had no idea what the hell he was doing. She was a drifter, just like Chloe.

It was insane.

Jessie's heartbeat jumped to answer his. 'Luke?'

'There's something about you…'

She held her breath as his head, mere inches from hers, tilted. Burnished slate eyes waited for her response.

'Intriguing. Very…'

This could only lead to heartbreak.

Move away.

Logic fled, leaving a void filled with hot temptation. Being with him was like having a luxurious treat.

Just one touch, one taste and she could leave, knowing how good it was to be in his arms.

Just once. Then she'd go. Definitely. Go.

Her eyes closed as his lips grazed hers.

A seagull screeched directly overhead.

'Oh.' She jerked in reaction, dragging her wits back to some semblance of sanity. Stupid. Nothing could come from this but pain and heartache.

She put space between them, folding her arms to create a barrier. 'We can't do this.'

'I know.' He thrust his hands in his pockets and tried to stanch the surge of heat racing through his body.

Really close shave.

He'd never thought he'd be so irritated and yet so grateful for a seagull's squawk. Another second and he'd have been in deep trouble.

His head cleared a little as his heartrate normalised. He shouldn't be there. He had responsibilities. He checked his watch. 'I need to go.'

Needed to walk away and not look back.

But she held his gaze, looking as ruffled and confused as he felt. 'Luke...'

'Look, Jessie, I'm sorry. It would be stupid to start anything.'

He watched her body relax. So she'd been fighting it too.

They needed some sort of agreement. Say it and then move on. 'We can only ever be friends. Nothing more. Seriously, we're going to be working together for just a few weeks and then you'll be gone.'

'I know. You're right.'

'So, do you want a ride home or take that walk?'

He couldn't look at her face, focused instead on the movement of her throat as she swallowed.

'I'll walk back.'

'Good. It's for the best.' Before she could answer he turned on the cooling sand and walked away, waiting for relief to flood through him.

It didn't come.

CHAPTER FOUR

A COOL evening breeze swathed Jessie as she hobbled towards the cul de sac, shoes in hand. The walk home along the gravel shoreside path might have ruined her feet, but it did her whirling mind a power of good.

Distance. That's what she needed. If she wasn't up close and personal with a problem, the problem didn't exist. Right?

And Luke McKenzie was definitely turning into a problem.

She turned the corner into the quiet street, trying to remember what sorry vestiges of food she had left in the fridge for dinner. Trying to forget how good it felt to be in his arms. Still waiting for the rush of relief at escaping with her emotions and her secrets intact.

She knew the pain of watching someone leave; their rush of shock at seeing her ugly scars, the tight stretch of their jaw and the empty silence after they'd left. It was a sound she had no desire to hear again. And only distance could prevent that.

'What the…?' Red flashing lights stopped her in her tracks. Her heart rate skittered, her legs quivered with the sudden surge of adrenalin.

She closed her eyes to steady herself as a video of blurred images bombarded her brain. The slick of rain on the road. The ear-splitting crash followed by an eerie silence.

Flashing red lights.

And the shiny shard of metal jutting from her abdomen.

Flashbacks. Forcing her eyes open, she shook her head. 'For God's sake, Jessie, forget the past. This is now.'

An ambulance outside Luke's house.

Luke. Lucy. Asthma.

Please let the little mite be okay. A surge of bile rose in her throat. She clamped it down and ran the last hundred metres to Luke's place.

From inside she heard a child's frantic screaming. Not breathless wheezing. A loud screech of fear. Or pain. A frightened child in the throes of an asthma attack wouldn't be able to make such a noise.

So please don't let her be hurt either. Or Luke.

'Luke! Are you okay?' Jessie flung the door open, scanned the hallway and followed a trail of red splatters, stark against the blond wood floorboards, towards the lounge. Her throat constricted. 'Oh. My. God. Luke!'

'Jessie.' Luke's voice, eerily flat compared to Lucy's intermittent wails, filled Jessie with dread.

Perched on the edge of a black leather sofa, left arm raised above his head by a paramedic, Luke gave her a weak smile. A deep slash ran from the base of his little finger to his thumb. Blood surged down his wrist and dripped from his elbow.

On one of Luke's knees sat a screaming, puce Lucy, who seemed to simultaneously want to hug his leg and crawl as far away from his bloody hand as she could. Poor wee thing. Jessie's heart pinched as she took her in properly for the first time. A frothy halo of wild curls, wide eyes and cute snub nose, bright red cheeks and a pout to die for. An angel, with a very loud voice.

'It's okay. I'm fine.' Luke pulled the little girl tight with his good arm and she snuggled against his chest, pacifier in mouth. Quietness descended on the house.

He kept his eyes on Jessie, serious and dark. She couldn't read him. Was he pleased she was here or still reeling, like she was, with the aftermath tsunami of questions of their near-miss kiss? Or had it meant nothing to him? Like it had with her ex, in the end.

The corner of Luke's lip twitched upwards. 'Sorry to give you a fright. Seriously, I'm okay. A word from the wise—never juggle with knives.'

'That wound looks nasty.' She nodded to the paramedic and dashed round the back of the sofa as a knot tightened in her stomach. A quick observation of Luke's colour and respiration rate told her he wasn't in shock. Yet.

But she was, surprised at the force of fear that had rippled through her when she'd thought either of them might be in danger. 'I'm Jessie, a doctor, and Luke's colleague. Do you mind if I take a look?'

'Hi, Jessie, I'm George. Sure.'

Having waited for George to step away, Jessie straightened Luke's palm, then curled it into a fist, feeling his hand twitch as blood poured from the gash.

'That needs exploring and a good number of stitches. Maybe even a hand surgeon referral. You might have cut a tendon. I could do a patch-up job, but I don't have the right equipment. I guess the ER isn't far away?'

'Fifteen minutes.' The paramedic smiled and bent to his equipment bag. 'Quicker with a red light.'

'We need a pressure dressing to stem the bleeding.'

'I'm right onto it.' George opened a sterile pack and pulled out a thick wad of gauze.

'Of course you are.' Jessie knelt in front of Luke, ignoring the sudden hitch in her heart at his tight smile. 'When I saw the ambulance I freaked. I thought it was Lucy and her asthma. What the heck were you doing?'

'I was cutting pineapple for Lucy's dessert and it sort of rolled. My hand slipped.'

'Since when have you been allowed access to sharp instruments? You really should leave that to the grown-ups,' she teased gently.

'Thanks for the sympathy.' The lines around his mouth looked more pronounced than earlier, but the spark in his eyes told her he'd got the joke. 'I wouldn't have called George out, but I didn't think I should drive my car.'

'Absolutely not.' She glanced at the dressing. A red tinge had bloomed on the white already. 'Shouldn't you be lying down? You could go into shock.'

He shook his head and nuzzled into Lucy's curls. 'No. It's fine. Seriously.'

George snapped his bag closed. 'I'll just head out and see what's happened to the other AO, he's probably radioing in. Then we'll get you to the ER.' He disappeared out the door.

Luke shrugged. 'I just wanted to share some dessert with Lucy. I'd missed her dinner. Becks, our childminder, cooks…' His pallor now matched the ivory scatter cushions on the sofa. 'We have a routine. Fixed. I don't miss dinner. We talk about our day.'

'Missed it…' *Because you were with me. And now you're hurt.*

See what happens when you get involved, Jessie. People get hurt. You get hurt. 'I'm sorry. We shouldn't have gone for that walk. That was my fault.'

'No. It was mine.' He edged forward on the sofa, shifting Lucy across his lap. 'And I shouldn't have been rushing once I got back here. My mind was on other things.'

The little scene at the beach? Yeah, right. *Not everything is about you.*

The little girl clung to him, sporadic sobs making her chest heave. He whispered into her ear and Jessie watched Lucy's lips slowly curl into a smile. The bond between the two of them was so strong. She was his world and he was hers.

A sharp jolt of envy jabbed Jessie's gut. Once she'd dreamed of having that kind of bond with a husband. A child. But now her world was entirely her own. She'd thought it was all she needed. Simple. Uncomplicated.

Keeping her distance was the price she paid to keep her heart and sanity intact. She'd been in the depths of darkness after her accident, after Michael had left, and had no rational desire to risk going there again. But being here with Luke and Lucy made her realise that, despite working her butt off around the world, she was lonely.

Luke stood and swung Lucy onto his hip, swaying slightly as the colour on his face morphed from ashen to green. 'Thanks for coming over. I appreciate it. Life gets difficult when things like this happen. I have no parents now, and no relatives close.'

'Of course. I want to help. Isn't that what neighbours do in an emergency?'

'Sure, Mary Poppins. You passed Childcare 101?' He took a wobbly step towards the door, his hand raised to stem the blood flow, and gave her a heart-melting smile. It shocked her that, after knowing him such a short time, just one look tipped her world sideways. Before they knew it they'd both be falling over.

'No, but I have a diploma in child health. And I know all the words to the odd nursery rhyme. If that counts.' She stuck an exasperated tongue out at him. 'Besides, this place is a disaster zone.'

She pointed to the blood stains on the floor, the rogue pineapple dripping juice over the fairy-festooned tablecloth in the open-plan lounge-diner. 'I'll clean up. And look after Lucy here. Otherwise, judging by the way she's gripping your arm, she'll have to be surgically removed before they can begin an examination under anaesthetic.'

Luke jerked Lucy higher on his hip. For a man losing blood at an alarming rate he was remarkably in control, masking his pain. Planning his world around his daughter.

'She's not good with strangers. I left a message on Becky's phone so hopefully she'll get it. Or I could ask Maggie to meet me at ER.'

'That makes no sense at all. She needs to stay here, keep to her routine, right?' Jessie tried to prise Lucy out of his arms, grasped the tiny tot's waist and pulled. The little girl shivered further under her dad's armpit and burst into tears. 'No.'

Jess bit back an unexpected rise of anxiety. Damn. She'd thought she'd got a lid on her emotions, but getting this close to a sobbing toddler sent tight shivers of sadness shocking through her.

A long time ago, in a Herculean effort to move forward she'd squashed all her mothering instincts to the darkest corner of her heart, never to be opened again. Had managed to cope with kids on a purely professional level. But the intimacy of dealing one to one with a screaming, desperate little girl scared her half to death. Could she do this?

She steeled herself. Luke needed her to do this. So did Lucy. She had to put whatever misgivings she had aside. 'Hey, why don't we read a book or play a game?'

'Are you sure?' Luke peeled Lucy's fingers from his shoulder, surprised by this turn of events. It was great to have the worry of Lucy taken care of, but having Jessie in his house could only complicate things. Heck, what choice did he have? He had to put Lucy first. Every time. And if that meant Jessie was in his house, then so be it. 'Thanks. I'm grateful for anything.'

But it was way too personal and then some. Especially after the encounter at the beach. They'd had a lucky escape and he'd planned to keep away from her, not have her in his space, leaving her scent and her larger-than-life presence here. The less time they spent together, the easier the next three weeks would be.

A sharp pain sliced his hand. Whatever. He needed to go before he fell over. Witnessing her father collapse certainly wouldn't be good for his daughter. 'Hey, Luce, this is Jessie, remember? She's my friend and she's going to look after you while a doctor makes my hand better. Jessie's very nice, you'll see.'

'No.' Lucy shook her head and hid under Luke's elbow. She began to cry, the jittery crescendo threatening a tantrum. How could a two-year-old's screaming send an adult man dangerously close to despair? But it did, every time. 'No! No! No!'

'Come on, Luce.' *I don't need this.* What he did need at times like this was another pair of hands. Another grown-up to share the load. Help. Struggling through it on his own was exhausting. Damned hard. 'She's my friend. She's fun, you'll see.'

Over the top of his daughter's head Jessie caught his stuck-on smile. Her cheeks burned as she remembered how close they'd come to kissing. And how much she'd wanted to do it.

His pale eyes flared, and she thought he must be remembering too, despite his daughter's tantrum. He mouthed the words '*See you later*' and a kaleidoscope of butterflies fluttered in her stomach. Hopefully between now and *later* she'd have summoned up a healthy dose of self-control.

'I'm nice. Really.' She dredged up a smile that she hoped would convince him his precious girl would be fine in her care. Then she firmly took hold of the squirming child. 'We'll be fine, won't we, squirt?'

'There's a list of contact numbers on the fridge. She needs her meds at bedtime, they're in the top drawer in the kitchen. Inhaler's in her room, she likes…'

'Go. Go! I can work it out. I might not be Mary Poppins, but I'm not the Wicked Witch of the West either. Blimey, it's late, she's tired. How hard can it be?'

Three long hours. *Bless the poor mite*. Jessie sighed and paced up and down the toddler's room in semi-darkness, cradling the sobbing girl in her arms. Luke was right. Lucy wasn't good with strangers. Jessie had tried pretty much everything she had in her limited armoury and nothing had worked. No matter how many times she'd tried to put Lucy onto the bed, she'd just clung tighter round Jessie's neck.

'You've got a heck of a lot of stamina for such a tiny thing.'

She slumped onto the fuchsia fairy bed, surveyed the room and shuddered. Way too much pink.

Maybe it was the raspberry walls distracting Lucy from sleep, or the whirling nightlight of cherry teddy bears making her queasy. Luke had probably thought he was doing the right thing, making it a little girl's paradise. But it gave Jessie a sugar rush just being there.

She whispered gently into Lucy's ear the way she'd seen Luke do it. 'Another story book? More milk?'

'N-n-no. Daddy. Daddy.'

'He'll come back soon. I promise.'

Lucy's long ragdoll-like limbs hung over Jessie's arms. There weren't even tears in those wide brown eyes now, just heart-wrenching dry sobbing. Ever since George had closed the door on the ambulance Lucy had cried, wailed, screamed, sobbed.

The phone ringing every half-hour didn't help. Luke appeared to have forgotten Jessie was a competent doctor, and his regular check-ups kept startling Lucy out of her almost drowsy state. In the end she'd had to tell him not to phone again as hearing his voice only made his daughter more upset.

'It's all right. He's getting his hand fixed, remember?' Jessie tried to whisper in a lullaby voice, but her own exhaustion seeped through. Or was it nerves? Could a child pick up on an adult's anxiety?

She adjusted her position, forced herself to relax. Perhaps Lucy sensed Jessie's unease from the pressure of her embrace. Maybe she was holding her too tightly, or not tightly enough.

This closeness to a child, so like how she'd imagined her own would be like, frightened her. It stirred a tender longing she'd thought she'd buried. A swell of sorrow clutched her chest. Squeezing Lucy closer, she breathed away the hurt. No use remembering things that had passed.

But she couldn't help wondering what kind of a mother she'd have made. Judging by her experience so far tonight, not a very successful one! Would she have been like Luke and stuck to discipline and routine, or been less rigid in her approach? One thing she knew most definitely, she'd have been nothing like her own mother.

As soon as she'd discovered she was pregnant Jessie had told her growing baby every day how much she loved it. Fussed over it. Cradled it. Played it music. She blushed at the memory, but the moment she'd felt those whispery kicks in response to Baby Mozart she'd known she had a musical protégée. A brain surgeon. A Nobel Prizewinner.

She'd held on tight to that bright light of hope that had connected her with her baby. Made a zillion promises she'd never had a chance to keep. And burned with love.

Michael had joked she'd have been a grade A

helicopter parent. Always hovering. But at least she'd have been one—a parent, that was.

Lucy's pursed lips sucked noisily around her dummy in feverish jerks. Eyelids drooped closed. Breathing stilled. Almost there…

Suddenly her eyes popped open, wide, searching. 'Want Daddy.'

'Hush, honey. Would you like this friend?' Jessie picked up a floppy velvet giraffe and tucked it into Lucy's fist.

'No. Daddy.' The toddler pointed a chubby finger to a collection of photographs next to the bed. In one, a young woman held a newborn close to her breast.

Chloe. Without a doubt. She had Lucy's snub nose and wide eyes, and a mass of wild hair. Pencil thin and dressed in a loose gypsy top, Chloe smiled dreamily. But even in a grainy photograph Jessie glimpsed the soft bohemian edge. A free spirit indeed. But at what cost her freedom?

In another photo the three of them grinned out, Luke cradling Lucy in one arm and the other tightly around Chloe. It was good for Lucy to have pictures of her mum. The child needed something tangible to hold onto, because she'd be too young to have real memories of her mother.

Sure, Lucy might not understand what had happened just yet. But one day she'd ask and Luke would have to tell her the story. Jessie only hoped his truth would be as sugar-coated as this room.

Her heart squeezed tight. Every child should believe they were wanted and loved by their parents. Especially this one.

Her thoughts flitted to her own mother, always the eminent geologist first. Wife second. Mummy... well, who knew where Jessie and Zac were on their mother's list of priorities? Throughout her children's lives Dr Marguerite Price had been distant and distracted, with her nose in a research paper, behind a closed door or out in the field.

Was it better to have a parent who abandoned you, or to co-exist with one who hardly acknowledged you were there? If *only* she'd had a chance, she'd have never let her child out of her sight.

She rocked Lucy while she stared at Luke's picture, at his honest eyes, his protective stance. He'd never abandon anyone. He was too busy collecting strays like Chloe. Despite what had happened, he'd created a good life. Lucy would be okay. Lucky tyke. And any other babies he had along the way. Because he would eventually have more. A man like Luke would be snatched up by any warm-blooded single woman with working ovaries.

'He's a looker, eh?' She hugged Lucy tighter. 'You lucky girl. He's hopelessly devoted to you.'

She scooped the photo up and placed it in Lucy's free hand. Sheesh, she'd be carrying half the contents of the room if she wasn't careful.

Creases formed across the toddler's forehead, her nose crinkled, her lips puckered. Another wail threatened. It seemed that where Lucy and Luke were concerned, separation anxiety was terminal.

'Daddy?'

'Oh-oh. Better keep moving.' The soothing seemed to work better when they were upright.

Scanning the room for a solution, she hit on the chink of darkness beyond the curtains. Maybe… just maybe.

She hoisted Lucy up into her arms and walked to the window. Through the curtains a bright crescent moon shimmered in a star-studded sky. 'See that? That's the man in the moon.'

'Yes?' The sobbing stilled. 'Man?'

'See his face there? The dark shadows and the light make up his face, he's smiling down at us because he wants us to go to sleep. He keeps us safe at night and he's happy when we're all tucked up in bed. We don't want to make the man in the moon sad, do we?'

'No.' The little girl shook her head seriously and frowned.

'And that place, the moon? I heard it's made of cream cheese. Yummy.' Jessie felt a little weird saying all this stuff, really, and she could barely remember the stories of her childhood. But it seemed to be working. She had Lucy's attention. The crying had stopped.

Pointing to a constellation of stars, Jessie continued, 'And there's the great hunter Orion. He's a very strong and brave man, just like your daddy. You can see his belt. There's his sword.' She traced the shape of the man and his sword on the window pane so that Lucy could see it. 'And there's the bull he's fighting.'

The froth of curls bobbed up and down as the wide eyes grew wider. 'A bull? In the sky?'

'Oh, yes, there are lots of animal shapes in the sky. But you have to be in different parts of the world to see them all. Dogs, a scorpion, a ram, a lion. And there's even a frying pan.'

'A pan?' Lucy giggled.

'For the man in the moon to cook food for all the animals, they have to eat something, silly.'

Jessie looked at the little girl's rapt face and sent silent thanks to her dad, who had entertained her with astronomy when she was little. At least one of her parents had managed to drag themselves away from competitive academia to pay attention to his children. However haphazard and brief.

One of her greatest pleasures on her travels had been staring at the night sky and tracing the constellations. She realised now that finding Orion and the Southern Cross had been her anchor, the only constant thing she could associate with her idea of home.

'And the brightest star in the sky is called Venus. Only it's not really a star, it's a planet. Venus was a very great lady, famous for love and beauty. Just like you will be one day.'

'You're funny.' Lucy laid her head on Jessie's shoulder and the corners of her lips curled around her dummy. Her tiny arms tightened around Jessie's neck, causing a lump to surge in her throat. Lucy's willingness to open her heart and trust humbled her. If only she could be as brave as this two-year-old.

'And you're clever-gorgeous.' Jessie rubbed her head against Lucy's, inhaling the sweet fragrance of bath bubbles and milk. With the comforting warmth of this little body and the smile blossoming in her soul, Jessie felt as though her heart might explode. And for the millionth time in three hours she tried to fathom what desperate part of a mother could leave her child. This child. This wriggling, giggling complexity of perfection.

'So, let's wave night-night to the man in the moon.'

Lucy raised a limp fist and waved to the moon. 'Night-night, Moon Man.'

They rocked for a few more moments, Lucy's breathing slowing, her body getting heavier. Eventually Jessie twisted round to look at the babe who still clutched her photo of Luke. 'Ah, finally asleep, with Luke.'

She laid the sleeping child under her super-bright pink duvet and tucked her in. Mission accomplished!

Slicking a kiss onto the tot's head, she crept to the door. 'Sleep tight, little one. At last.'

Then she crawled into the nearest bed and tried to blot out the thought that she was leaving in nineteen days. And hoped separation anxiety wasn't contagious.

CHAPTER FIVE

HAVING checked on Lucy first, Luke stood at the doorway of his bedroom, watching the gentle rise and fall of Jessie's ribs. 'So, you *can* be quiet. Who would have known?'

Her flowery scent filled the room. Mussy light blonde-green hair contrasted sharply with the dark navy pillows, creamy skin he ached to touch, the gentle pout and little snorey noises. Stunning.

He should leave now.

However, unable to help himself, he stepped further into the room and enjoyed this moment of peace.

The missed kiss at the beach bothered him. More than he'd thought it would. How many stolen kisses had he had in his life? Dozens.

So why had this one been special? He was damned if he knew, but they'd been on the edge of something daring and wild. The first mad thing he'd done in years. It had certainly been a risk. A stupid risk.

A lucky escape.

'Luke?' Her voice was thick with sleep as she stirred, rubbing her hair, her face. Her hand darted to her stomach and she dragged the duvet up to her chin, then flicked on a side-lamp and squinted. 'Back already?'

He'd reached the threshold, acting nonchalant, imagining what it would be like to lie next to her. *God.* He leaned against the doorframe and flailed around for some perspective. He was tired. Surely, after a few hours' shut-eye, he'd see things differently. But right now he had to get the lowdown on his daughter.

He whispered across the semi-darkness. 'Hey, Mary Poppins. How's it going?'

'I've had two hours' sleep, I'm in a strange man's bed, still in yesterday's gloop.' *Strange* man? Six-thirty in the morning and she had all guns blazing. 'How's it sounding to you so far?'

'My mistake. You are so not Mary Poppins. I think I preferred you asleep.' He grinned. My, she was feisty. 'Being in any bed sounds good to me, even fully clothed. They have got to do something about those hospital waiting times. I sat for hours twiddling my thumbs. Well, the one thumb I was able to twiddle.'

Her head jerked up. 'Is your hand okay? What happened?'

He held up his thickly bandaged palm in a fresh white sling. 'No real damage. Thirteen stitches and a tetanus booster for good measure. They sure like to get their kicks with needles at that place.'

She smiled as she sat up and curled her legs over the edge of the bed. 'Thank your lucky stars it wasn't me. I'd have used a much bigger bore.'

'And no anaesthetic. Yeah, I know.'

Even at the crack of dawn she had a sense of humour. Chloe had always been a late riser and uncommunicative until after her first caffeine shot. Chloe…funny how he'd shoved her to the back of his mind for months, years, and yet now held Jessie up in comparison to her.

So different, but in reality very similar. Chloe had left. Jessie was leaving. There was a warning there somewhere. *Listen to it.*

Down the corridor Lucy let out a little sleepy cry.

'Hush. Don't wake her.' He edged back into his room, closing the door, and immediately regretted the intimacy that created. But he had Lucy to think about too. His number-one priority, he had to put her needs first. Plus, he didn't want his daughter to see Jessie in his bed. That would be too freaky.

'If she wakes too early, she'll be cranky. How

was last night? Did she settle in the end? Did you give her more milk? Asthma okay?'

'As I told you in your first, second and third phone calls, she didn't cough once. It was a breeze.' Jessie waved a hand in the air. The movement tightened her blouse across her breasts, transfixing him.

He reluctantly dragged his gaze upwards. 'I was concerned. I don't leave her often.'

'I understand, but by the third call I was getting a bit irritated.'

'Really? I didn't notice. Honestly, it took me weeks to get her to sleep at a regular time.'

'Then I did it in record time. Just call me the Toddler Whisperer.'

'You're kidding me?'

'Yes.' Massaging fingers along her temple she gave a slight nod. 'I'm so not used to restless nights. I don't know how you do it. How on earth did you manage after Chloe left?'

Luke sighed, remembering the endless hours of pushing Lucy's buggy through the dark streets, trying to get her to sleep. Trying to bring some semblance of normality into her disrupted life. 'Phenergan.'

'You gave a child sleeping medicine?' she gasped.

'No, that was for me.' He laughed at the shock

on her face. 'You're way too easy to wind up. Truthfully, it was hard but we stuck to a routine and wore each other down. I had no choice. She slept eventually.'

Reaching into his wardrobe with his good hand, he grabbed his shirt and trousers, pretending it was normal to chat to a beautiful woman as he got ready for the day. Even in the short time Chloe had been around she'd never talked much in the mornings. Or much at all really, unless it had been to complain or jibe.

Jess straightened out her crinkled clothes. She looked so much better mussed up. He wanted to muss her up all over again. He mentally shook himself.

She was doing him a neighbourly favour. Not a sexual one. Say thanks and move on.

Her lips curved back into that oddly distracting smile. 'Parenting sounds really hard.'

'It has its stressful moments. There's so much to think about. What she needs, if she's happy. Has she got friends, is she hitting her milestones? Does she miss her mum? The list goes on. But it's magic watching her grow into a little person.'

'Can I be honest? I'm not surprised she can't fall asleep in that bedroom—it's like living inside a stick of rock candy.'

He nodded, mesmerised by the movement of her hand combing through her wild hair. The tiny pout as she frowned in concentration over a knot or split end.

He pulled himself together.

'Pink overkill? I did wonder. I'll tone it down when I get a chance. I thought pink was a girl thing.'

'Sleeping Beauty would have trouble falling asleep in there.' Her eyes darted to the door as she spoke. He got the impression she was making a strategic calculation of how quickly she could leave.

He ran a hand across his stubbled chin and was reminded he needed a shave. He checked his watch. Timing was critical for a smooth transition to work. For their routine. 'Look, sorry, I need to get ready.'

She nodded purposefully. 'Me too. I'm going.'

'Great. Thanks again. So much.' He slipped his hand out of the sling, then tried to unhook the sling from his neck. And failed. He tried again. And failed. 'Damned thing, it's like wrestling in a straitjacket.'

'Here, let me help.' In an instant Jessie was in front of him, reaching up to untangle his limbs.

Little sighs of air, like butterfly kisses, escaped

her lips as she went up on tiptoe to wind the sling from his neck. 'Come closer. Bend down a bit, that's right.'

He dipped his head to inches away from her chest and her silky skin. From this angle he caught a glimpse of her white lace bra and the swell of her breasts.

The essence of flowers intensified. Suddenly the room temperature notched up a few degrees. She had an adorable frown of concentration. Sleep creases round her eyes. In the old wild days of his youth he'd have whipped her into his arms and made love to her right there. Then walked away, his heart unscathed. But he restrained himself, the saintly part of him wresting with the devil, and winning. This time. But for how long? It would be far better all round if she left.

Jessie dropped the sling onto the bed, those dark eyes blinking up at him. 'There you go, but keep that arm elevated to stop any more swelling.'

He swallowed hard. She was standing so close. In his bedroom. In lace underwear. He started to feel woozy again. 'Thanks, Jess. Expertly done. And now I need help to unbutton my shirt.'

'I don't think so.' Her pupils flared dark and wide, as her tongue moistened her half-closed lips.

He knew she felt the same zing of energy between them, could literally see her body reacting to him.

She took a step back at the same time he did. 'If you need a hand with Lucy later, just shout.'

Lucy. Yes, focus on Lucy. His entire life was about focusing on Lucy. Was it wrong to wish your child was asleep just for the moment so you could seduce a beautiful woman?

He didn't want to know the answer. 'Lucy's fine. She's fast asleep.'

He paused. *What the hell.* 'So you could stay, help me with my shirt, and then I could help you with yours.'

Had his brain to mouth pathways malfunctioned? What exactly was he suggesting?

Judging by the flash of heat in her eyes, Jessie knew exactly what he was suggesting. She tapped her index finger on his top button and flicked it. 'Not a hope in hell, buster. I'm going home. Right now. I have a clinic to do and I've a hunch the boss will be off sick so it'll be busy.'

Her gaze shifted to the clothes he'd hung on the en suite doorhandle. She started to get that grumpy frown again. The one she'd had…well, pretty much since he'd met her.

'Whoa. What the heck do you think you're doing?' she demanded.

'Other than trying to undress you, I'm getting my gear ready for the day,' he said.

She shook her head. 'You're not going to work today?'

'Sure am.'

She rekindled her guerilla killer stance—hands on hips, full-blown defiance in her eyes. 'How many hours' sleep did you have?'

'A few, on and off.'

'Not enough to deal with sick patients. You need a clear head. And what painkillers did they give you?'

'A local, paracetamol if needed. Which it isn't. I'm good to go. Besides, I probably had more sleep than you.'

'But I'm not in pain.'

He looked for the steam coming out of her ears and smiled as sweetly as he could. 'Bless you for caring.'

'Says who? Fine, go to work.'

'How about I get Lucy ready, come in for the morning and see how I feel? I'm a professional, there's no way I'd put any of my patients at risk. Now, if you could just…'

He eased his top button undone with theatrical difficulty. Even though dangerous, he couldn't resist the mix of horror and excited sparkle in her face. Playing with her was fun. Wicked. He hadn't done wicked in a very long time. He decided to up the stakes. 'Maybe you could elevate my arm while I shower?'

'I'm sure you'll manage. I'll see you outside in an hour or so.' Jessie made it to the door, barely managing to control her stuttering breathing. As if waking up in his bed wasn't bad enough. The smell of him caught up in her hair, on her clothes, pervading her senses. Taking hold.

Now he was asking her to undress him. And sending her good intentions spiralling out of control. Thoughts of him in the shower swirled in her addled mind. She stopped at the doorway. 'Won't your bandage get wet?'

'Your dedication to your patients is unsurpassed, Jess. Changed your mind about joining me in there?'

'You wish.'

'Okay, the frown speaks volumes. I'll get a bin liner to protect it.'

His hand stalled on the second button. A small triangle of tanned muscle was visible underneath the fabric of his shirt. His shoulders flexed as he moved, tensing and relaxing when he laughed. What would it be like to run a hand across that skin? To feel him under her fingertips?

For goodness' sake, surely it was too early in the morning to have such thoughts?

'Wait here, I'll go get the bag.' If she didn't get out right now she'd do something she'd regret. Like bypass the damned buttons and just rip his shirt off.

Think of something else. The sound of a tap running steered her thoughts.

Like him in the shower. No, not that again.

She ran downstairs gulping in air, and scrabbled in his cupboards for something to wrap around his hand.

Distance. *Keep. Your. Distance. Remember?*

Between the kitchen and the bedroom she'd affirmed her next moves. Protect his hand. Retreat. Go home. Protect…

In order not to wake Lucy, Jessie tiptoed back upstairs, pushed open Luke's bedroom door and paused, sucking in a deep breath.

Humming quietly, with his back to her, unaware she was there, Luke slipped his trousers down well-toned hips. His quads rippled as he shucked his garments off. A wide expanse of knotted shoulder muscle eased as he straightened. This was a guy who clearly looked after his body.

Then, slowly…very, very slowly…he turned.

It seemed like minutes as she took in taut limbs,

smooth skin over a flat plane of stomach, a fine line of hair from his belly button to the top of low-slung underwear.

'You like what you see, Jess?'

She struggled to get air into her lungs. She was all out of quips. She wanted so much to touch him. And wanted him to touch her. 'Yes,' she said boldly.

'Me too.' He edged closer. 'Very much. Come here, Jess.'

Her heart rate jittered.

Walk. One foot. Then the other. Walk away.

Reluctantly, she dragged her line of sight upwards, past the belly button, to the hard chest wall that rose and fell in increasing speed, to the Adam's apple that dipped sensually as he swallowed.

The room shrank to the tiny space that held the two of them, suffocatingly close in a smog of early morning heat.

'Stop calling me Jess.'

'Stop frowning, Jessie.' He reached his unbandaged hand towards her, his playful spark cementing into something much more serious. 'Come here, *Jessica*.'

The way he whispered her name with a velvet purr almost undid her. No one, not even Michael, had evoked such intense desire—and she'd been married to him. Before...before the accident.

'No, I can't. I told you.' Her mouth dried as she traced her vision upwards to his full, slightly parted lips, the sharp cheekbones, the intense gaze that asked her so many questions, and offered her so many promises, so much hope.

Low in her abdomen every cell she had left came alive, every nerve charged. She didn't need hope, she needed a miracle.

'Here's your liner. I have to go.' Her voice was forced over the hoarseness in her throat. She threw the bin bag onto the bed. 'We're going to be late for work. And we don't want that, do we?'

He took a step nearer, a spice scent that was all man and all Luke filling the air around them. 'I'm the boss. I can do what I like.'

'For God's sake, save us both and tell me to go.'

'Go.'

His fingers touched her arm, tracing slow circles towards her shoulder, and her breath stalled in her chest. Hard hips brushed against her, like a magnet pulling her to him.

'Get out now, Jessie, if you want.' His eyes flicked down her body. 'Before it's too late.'

He was smiling, a wicked glint in his eye, his breathing erratic. His brows raised in expectation.

Speaking was impossible.

Thinking was impossible.

She forced words out. 'I…I should…'

There'd been enough time to turn away.

Enough time to gather long lost wits.

And enough time to hear the patter of feet along the corridor.

'Daddy!' The door shoved open, revealing a grinning Lucy who dashed over to Luke and hugged his leg. 'Daddy's home.'

He jumped away from Jessie and swooped up his daughter, wincing slightly as she settled on his sore hand. 'Great timing, little one.'

'All better.' Lucy placed her palms on his cheek and kissed his lips.

Great timing indeed. Finally the trembling stemmed as Jess breathed out deeply. They'd come way too close for comfort. She had to put a stop to this. Leave.

A frown gathered over Lucy's brows as she peered towards the daylight. 'Jess, Moon Man gone?'

'Yes, sweetie. It's his turn to go to bed now. He'll be there looking after you again tonight. So you have to be good and go to sleep straight away.'

It was Luke's turn to frown. 'Moon Man?'

'Long story. But it works a treat.' She winked

at him. 'I might just let you into our secret if you ask me nicely.'

'Oh, believe me, Jessie, I can be nice.' Wanton promise flared in his eyes. 'Very nice.'

'I bet you can.' She held his gaze for a second. Two seconds. Three.

And then realised she was flirting again. It was instinctive with him. Annoying. Sending totally the wrong message. Especially at six-thirty in the morning.

Any man could be *nice* when he wanted something. Michael had been spectacular at wooing. Pretty accomplished at rejecting too. But when she'd needed support, well, he'd just about fallen over his own feet to escape. She needed to steer away from *nice*.

'I really do need to go home. And you need a shower.' She shrugged. 'Perhaps a cold one would be good.'

'The invitation still stands.' His eyebrows rose as he kept right on looking at her. He smiled lazily, a come-to-bed smile, an I-want-you-smile. A *later* smile. The trembling came back with force. She swallowed hard as she watched his mouth moving. Wanting to trace her fingers along those lips.

'But you're right, Jessie. Stupid idea.'

He refocused on Lucy, tickled her ribs, and she

squirmed in his arms. Infectious giggles filled the air.

Suddenly the room felt larger again, bright light filtered through the blinds and fresh air filled Jessie's lungs. Although the sight of Luke naked, apart from a pair of snug undies and cuddling a child, made her ache with longing for what she would never have.

Lucy pointed at Jessie. 'Jess, you havin' breakfast?'

'No, sweetheart, I need to go home.'

'*Jessie*,' Luke told his little girl. 'She gets cross if you call her Jess. But I think it suits her.'

'Seems like there's a general move for me to be Jess. Okay, okay, call me Jess if it makes you happy.' Grateful for the distraction from Luke's torso, Jessie smiled and ruffled Lucy's manic locks. 'Just don't blame me when Lucy realises all the other Jesses in the world are cats. Or cows. I couldn't bear the comparison.'

'Unlikely.' Luke's pupils flared, warming her. 'Very unlikely.'

'Okay, I'm definitely going now. Got to get out of these stinky clothes.'

She waved to them from the doorway. How could it be possible to be desperate to leave and yet yearning to stay?

The guy looked cute, okay. Nothing more. Just her raging hormones getting the better of her. 'Bye, Lucy. Bye, Luke.'

But it struck her with a force, as she got halfway down the stairs, that it wasn't lust or hormonal imbalance or celibacy or any other lame excuse she could throw at her body's reaction to his touch. It wasn't his hot abdomen, his wicked smile, his sense of humour.

It was all of those things and more. He was a good man. A kind man. An honest man.

The next three weeks were going to test her resolve to the limits.

CHAPTER SIX

'YOU are *not* going to drive this car.' Jessie leaned back against the driver's door of Luke's precious Audi and folded her arms, glaring at him with a force that whipped his breath away. Her hair swirled in the early morning breeze, and she wore another too-grown-up blouse. This one was rose-coloured, matching the slick of lipstick on the taut line of her lips.

Fleetingly, he wondered what it tasted like.

Hell, he'd managed nearly sixty minutes of solid focus on Lucy and the day ahead. Now look, crazy-teenager thoughts had crept in once again. He really did need to control his fickle hormones and get to work. That little bedroom scene earlier had been fun. But fun didn't tend to his daughter, fun didn't pay the bills and fun didn't protect his heart.

'For God's sake, move out of the way, Jessie. We're getting nowhere fast—other than late for work. And Lucy's going to miss the kindergarten zoo trip.'

Jessie was immovable. 'You must be the only man in New Zealand with a manual gearbox, and you're not safe to drive it with an injured hand.'

She poked her finger at him. 'Anyway, how come Lucy's at the zoo today? Where's Becky?'

'Day off. It's good for Lucy to mix with other kids. Until she gets siblings of her own.'

Beside him Jess stiffened. She bit her lip and twisted down to wave at Lucy through the back window. Shadows edged her eyes, and once again she wore a haunted expression. Probably something to do with the impending journey to work. She seemed strangely spooked by cars. As if she'd ever admit it.

'How about I drive?' She held out her hand.

'No.' Reaching into his pocket, he snagged his palm on his belt buckle. Shivers of pain sliced through his hand and he felt the spread of ooze sticking on the bandage. Okay, so driving was a bad idea. 'We could walk.'

'What? And let Lucy miss her trip? Not on my watch.' She pressed her upturned hand towards him, her jaw rigid. Her free hand palmed her belly. 'Give me the keys.'

'No.'

'Why not?'

'Just no.'

'Not good enough. Let me drive.'

'No.'

'Why the hell not?' She flashed him a look that dared him to deny her.

Because I can see the nervous guarding of your stomach. Staccato gulps of breath. You don't want to drive. You don't want get into the car at all.

'Because you're not insured for my car.'

'I have a licence. And we will actually get to work in one piece.' She didn't say the words *I hope.* But they hung in the silence.

He hesitated to let her do something that so obviously freaked her. He was supposed to be the hero, not her. 'Look, Jess, you've been great, but you don't have to help me any more. We'll get a cab.'

'You started it.'

'What?'

'The helping thing.' She blinked up at him, resignation in the curve of her lips. 'You sorted out Zac's pool. You bathed my eyes. You help people all the time. Now it's my turn. So, for God's sake, give me the keys.'

'What choice do I have?'

'None.' She looked like she was trying to convince herself as well as him. 'We have patients waiting and that poor girl in the back needs to see a tiger or two before the day is out.'

'Okay. Thanks. I owe you, big time.' He held the car door open for her. 'Er, you do know how to drive a manual?'

'Yep, it's like riding a bike. One of those things you never forget. Unfortunately.' Chewing a corner of her bottom lip, she wiggled the key into the ignition. Her hands trembled as she gripped the wheel. She closed her eyes and breathed deeply. 'Right, let's go.'

'You okay?'

'Yep.'

'You want to talk about it?'

'No.' Her eyes flashed to the rear-view mirror, once, twice, then she slipped the car into first and stuttered to the intersection. 'Now, don't talk.'

'Clear my side.' Luke glanced in both directions and saw a solitary car coming towards them hundreds of metres away. 'Plenty of time.'

'I mean it. If you're going to comment the whole time then you can get out now. I'll drop Lucy at crèche on my own.'

'Sorry, I'll shut up.'

'Good.'

She waited until the car had eased passed them. Then waited again, checked both directions and edged slowly onto the highway. A sheen of sweat gathered over her top lip, she hunched forward in her seat, only briefly snatching her hand off the steering-wheel to change gear.

Ahead of them stretched an open road. But behind them snaked a long line of traffic hedging across the central reservation, flashing and tooting and trying to overtake her. She stuck to fifty. Not a kilometre over or a kilometre less.

Finally they swung into the crèche car park and Jessie heaved a huge sigh. She sat back and wiped her hands across her stomach. Turning to him, she smiled. 'There we go. Took a bit longer than usual, but here safe and sound. And if you ever talk to me while I'm driving again, I swear I'll pull your stitches out with my teeth.'

Her voice had taken on a high pitch, wavering a little. She swallowed. Appeared to gain control. 'So, better get to work, then. I'll walk from here. Leave the car, I'll get it later. Have a good time at the zoo, lucky Lucy.'

She jumped out of the seat, popped a kiss on Lucy's head and rushed off down the road.

Luke watched her with a new-found respect, aware of the huge toll that short drive had taken on her. She was full of guts, that woman.

Even more now he wanted to ask what made her so scared of driving, the nervous hand-over-belly thing, but he didn't know how. It seemed too intrusive. He doubted she'd tell him anyway, probably just stab him with a scalpel if he dared to ask.

He didn't like it that he'd been so helpless. Didn't like it that she'd had to step in and drive them.

But like it or not, Jessie had put herself on the line, pushed herself beyond the edge of her comfort zone. Not just this morning, but last night too. For him. For Lucy.

The more he got to know her, the more she intrigued him.

Damn it.

'There's no pulse. Get the defib, Maggie. Quick.' Jessie took her fingers away from the carotid artery of the old man lying across the entrance of the surgery. Then straightened him and ripped open his shirt to access his chest.

'Call an ambulance. Get hold of Luke. And get rid of this audience.' She nodded towards the knot of people by the doorway. 'It's not a reality TV show.'

Bending to his bluish lips, she listened for breath sounds. Nothing. Cripes. What a way to start her lunch hour.

'Danger. Response. Airway. Breathing. Circulation,' she reminded herself.

Easy as DR ABC.

Kneeling at the old guy's head, she tilted his chin up and back. Swept a finger across his airway. Pinched his nose and blew deeply twice into his mouth. Relief rippled through her as his chest rose and fell with her breaths.

She crawled to his side, knotted both hands into a tight fist and positioned them over his heart. 'Here goes, mate. One. Two. Three.'

Counting aloud maintained her focus as she pushed hard and fast onto his ribcage, feeling the dip and give of his bones with every stroke. 'Fifteen. Sixteen. Where's Luke?'

Despite her need to put space between them, she'd feel better with him around. *Since when*?

He was a damned fine doctor. *Obviously*. Easy explanation. Even though she was perfectly capable of dealing with this on her own, CPR was simply easier with two. One to blow, one to pump.

Forcing him out of her head, she continued to pump with straight arms, transmitting all her life force into this poor man. Willing him to survive. Somewhere he'd have a family that loved him, who would feel the pain of losing him.

'Losing you?' she exhaled. 'Not today, mate.'

Tingling through her body alerted her to Luke's arrival. The resus trolley clattered behind him and unwitting relief flooded through her. He could take his share of the CPR load now.

Sure. Like that was the only reason her heart jumped at the sight of him.

With defib in hand, he knelt next to her and smiled. 'Can't leave you alone for five minutes without a drama.'

He applied two large sticky pads to their patient's chest. 'Maggie's on the phone, she'll be right back.'

Then he searched Jessie's face. 'You okay?'

'Yep. One. Of. Yours?' She continued pumping.

He stared hard at the old guy's face. 'Don't think so. ID?'

'Haven't. Checked.' She dragged in a breath, another one. 'Twenty-two. Twenty-three. Stumbled into the surgery. Twenty-six. Clutching his chest. Collapsed.'

'Any kind of pulse?'

'Not that I can get. Thirty.' Rocking back on her heels, she drew the back of her hand across her forehead. 'Man, that's hard. What's the reading?'

They paused for the automated external defibrillator to interpret the heart rhythm. A wobbly line appeared on the LED.

'VF.' Jessie stared at the screen and waited for instructions.

A mechanical voice bellowed into the silence. 'Preparing shock. Move away from patient.'

They scrambled back and watched as the old guy's body jerked under the force of sharp electrical current, then slump again.

Silently, Jessie willed a readable trace, her heart maintaining its own wild rhythm.

'When instructed, begin compressions,' the artificial drone continued.

'How cool are these machines? CPR for dummies.' Luke handed her an ET tube and laryngoscope. 'Any chance you can intubate?'

'Sure.'

'Great. I'll pump.'

'Wow. All mod cons here. I didn't have this luxury in Vietnam.' Jessie slipped the laryngoscope into the man's throat, guided the breathing tube into his trachea, connected an ambu-bag and gave two long blasts of portable oxygen.

'Slick. Well done.' Luke smiled in appreciation. 'Straight in first time. Not too shabby.'

'Impressive, eh?' Her heart swelled with pride. She'd done that procedure countless times before and no one had ever made her feel so good about it. She caught his intent gaze, felt the heat of the potent charge zapping between them. Only the slightest ignition would have it raging out of control.

If you don't play with fire you won't get burnt.

'Ready for round three?' He nodded down at the patient and knotted his hands. Began rapid thrusts onto the man's chest in rhythm with the automaton's counts.

'Give it all you've got.' She counted with him, clawed back some control.

When he reached thirty she blasted two more bursts of oxygen and then waited again for the shock.

Still no response from the man. Jessie again willed him to breathe, prayed for a flicker of a heartbeat. 'Come on. Don't give up on us yet, mister.'

'When instructed, give compressions,' the robotic voice repeated.

'Okay, okay. I'm onto it.' Luke placed the heel of his palm on the man's chest and pumped again, his muscles tightening and relaxing with every movement. 'Come on, mystery man, breathe for me.'

Out of the corner of her eye Jessie recognised George, the paramedic from yesterday, sidle up next to her.

Had it only been last night? It seemed like she'd known Luke a lifetime, but it was only a handful of shifts in George's working life. A few hours. Of

utter chaos, jumbled emotions and awakened desire. Her life would never be the same again.

She squeezed oxygen into the man's lungs twice
more. Again they waited for the machine's verdict.

'When instructed, give compressions.'

Then, 'Rhythm changed, shock cancelled.'

When Luke pressed a finger to their patient's
neck he beamed. 'A pulse? Fantastic.' His smile
slipped. 'Very faint and all over the place. But a
pulse nonetheless.'

'Wow! Great! Now keep going.' Jessie nodded
and bit back a smile. Her veins pulsed with relief
and exhilaration. The old man was still in grave
danger, but they'd beaten the awful odds and re-
started his fibrillating heart. That had to be worth
celebrating.

Thirty minutes later, Jessie waved the ambulance
off to a more suitable environment for an intubated patient.

Luke appeared by her side. 'His name is Harold
Jenkins. Here on holiday. His wife's meeting him
at A and E.'

'Good luck, Harold.' Jessie sighed deeply as the
ambulance disappeared round the corner. 'I guess
we should go inside and get ready for the afternoon session.'

'Just a second. I need some fresh air.' He walked to a picnic table overlooking the bay, his dark eyes sincere with muted excitement. 'Enjoy the peace while we can.'

Her heart stumbled as she sat opposite him, unsure what to say.

Certainly not to make intimate conversation, but there was always a need to de-stress after an intense experience, to help calm the nerves and create an improved pathway for next time.

'Mr Jenkins,' she said, 'was on the brink of death and we dragged him back.'

'We did. We make a good team.'

'Hell, yes. A damned fine team. Like a well-oiled machine.'

His lips curved into a grin that she suddenly wanted to kiss.

No. She couldn't. They'd agreed not to get involved. Especially not when there was a child involved too. Too much to want. Too much to leave. Too much potential for fresh hurt.

But she couldn't help feeling pride from his compliments. He made her feel respected. Valued—he took time out to talk to her, to thank her for the small things. And the fire in his eyes made her feel desirable for the first time in for ever.

Damn him, he was starting to make her *feel*

things and she didn't want to feel at all. Her palm rested briefly over her stomach, felt the dips and ridges of her scars. Remembered the pain she'd endured and survived. She'd *felt* enough to last her a lifetime.

Luke continued, the adrenalin still evident in his animation, 'Every time a patient survives CPR it's like a miracle. It's brilliant. Makes you realise how fragile life is.'

She knew that well enough. 'After every CPR I promise myself I'll try to live a little better, be a bit braver.'

And then soon enough she'd be back to her old ways, adding more bricks to that protective wall she kept on building.

'Braver? You're the bravest woman I've met.' He smiled. 'Well, the scariest anyway.'

'Little ol' me?' She bit her lip, trying not to stare at Luke's face and snatch that rogue kiss she'd been thinking about. Now, that would be brave. And brainless. But, oh, so lovely. 'Do you have arrests here a lot? It's a bit dramatic for a small town surgery.'

'First one.' His brows lifted. 'You were great.'

'Those AED machines are very cool. Just follow the *rob-ot-ic co-mmands*.' She emphasised the last words in the dull monotone of the machine.

He laughed. 'I. Didn't. Just. Mean. The. Resus.'

'You sound more like a Dalek than an AED. Don't give up the day job.'

'I know. Bad, eh?'

He dropped the mimicry. The colour of his eyes changed to an intense dark grey as his face grew serious. He seemed about to stand up, hesitated, then settled back in his seat.

'I should thank you for driving this morning. I get the impression it was a big call for you.'

Here we go. How about that protective wall loses a few bricks? Take a risk and talk? She dragged in a breath. *Feel?*

'Yes, I'm just about okay as a passenger, but getting behind the wheel rattles me. I had a prang a few years back. It shook me up a bit.'

'And you were okay? Did you get hurt?' His face filled with a concern that was deeply touching. 'Now I think about it, Zac did mention something a while ago. I was so strung out with Lucy it passed me by.'

'It was nothing much, just a few scrapes. No big drama.'

'There's always drama in a car crash, Jess.' He scanned her face, but she looked away as she clamped down on the pain brimming to the surface.

She was briefly tempted to tell him everything. To unburden herself of the weight she'd been carrying. But that kind of conversation would put such a downer on their friendship. She'd worked hard to move on. It was old news. Only recently had it reared its head a little—when holding Lucy, or trying to resist Luke's charms.

He smiled. 'Sounds like you had a hard time.'

'Stuff happens. I'm fine now.' *Don't pity me.*

He nodded but said nothing further.

It seemed he understood not to pry too deeply, allowed her to leave the subject and not ask too many questions. For that, at least, she was grateful.

'One thing, though.' His head tilted to one side as he squinted in the bright sunshine.

She tried to stay calm. 'I hate out-of-the blue questions.'

'How come there's no Mr Jessie? Never been tempted to settle down?'

'Once. It's ancient history. We worked together, lived together. Got married. Didn't work out. Very messy. One thing I learnt—don't get involved with people at work.' She winked. 'Word is he's married now with a baby on the way.'

That was as far as she needed to go. Remembering, feeling things hurt too much. 'I went back on the road after we broke up. I don't have time for a relationship, I'm always on the move.'

'I suppose it makes things difficult.'

Luke shuddered in frustration. What was difficult was trying to ignore this weird draw to her and steer the conversation away from such personal things. He didn't want to talk about his life with her. He should be grateful she didn't appear overly keen to share her history with him either. He didn't want to connect, or share.

Every time he tried to create a barrier she knocked it down with her humour, her kindness, her strength. And those pouty lips he couldn't get out of his brain.

He didn't like it. Not at all. The sooner he went back to work, the sooner he could fill his head with things other than her. Or at least try. He stood up and touched her sleeve. 'Come on, we'd better get back to the patients.'

When he lifted his hand from her arm, his heart pounded in disbelief. 'Oh, God, I'm sorry.'

CHAPTER SEVEN

JESSIE peered at her sleeve and recoiled.

A thick red smear covered the diameter of her upper arm. 'Oh, my goodness. Your hand.'

'It was the CPR.' He held it up and grimaced. The bandage hung limply in ribbons around his wrist. 'I'll get Maggie to take a peek.'

'Like hell you will.'

Jessie dragged him back to the surgery and into a treatment room, aware of the now familiar surge of concern swirling around her gut.

For goodness' sake, she had to stop this innate knee-jerk reaction to him. 'Ask Maggie, indeed. I'm pretty good at suturing. Top of the class at med school. Sit down.'

She shook her head as she held a chair out for him, grabbed the dressing trolley and bent over his outstretched hand. 'It's been a heck of a day. And this is not helping.'

'I love it when you're angry,' he whispered. 'Your eyes spark and your lips form a tight line.

You look like you're going to explode. You think you're holding it all in, but every emotion is written across your face.'

'I am not angry, I'm concentrating,' she breathed as she unwound the sticky mess of bandage and dressing that covered his hand. Her heart hammered. Could he really see what she was thinking? Lordy, she'd have to be careful. 'Am I so transparent?' she couldn't help asking.

'Yep. Like glass. Only a sight sharper.' He smiled, allowing a glimpse of straight white teeth. His smile faded as she probed the loosened stitches.

'Painful?'

He flinched as she probed deeper. 'No.'

'Liar.' His pale face belied his cool demeanour. She pursed her lips. Then plastered on a smile of her own, trying to confuse him with her so-called transparency. She'd show him what a closed book she could be. 'You've burst five stitches. So, okay, I'm frustrated. You should have been more careful. I could have done the compressions while you intubated.'

'I know. But compressions are hard work.'

'You thought I couldn't manage the compressions? Is that it?' She struggled with her mask of impartiality and downgraded the massive urge to hit him to a small swat on his arm.

'Hell, no. I was trying to help. We saved the guy's life. Besides...'

'What?'

'Now I get to spend more time with you.'

'Watch it.' She swatted him again and her cheeks reddened.

He winced. This time it was his smooth line and not the pain. Seemed every time he opened his mouth he couldn't help sparking some comment. Better to concentrate on her intense focus, the little frown above the bridge of her nose. The tiny glimpse of lace as she bent over his hand. The tight pout of those kissable lips.

And keep his mouth shut.

Actually, better not to focus on her at all.

He closed his eyes and tried to think of anything other than being here and that flowery smell. Unfortunately, the top ten famous All Blacks didn't cut it. Her scent kept pulling him back to this room. To her mouth. To her.

He couldn't kiss her. He'd made a promise. Had agreed to be friends, nothing more. Anything else would be just senseless.

But it didn't stop him wanting to.

He'd need every ounce of willpower to get out of this room without giving in to the urge to plant a kiss on those smart lips.

'Is it sore?' Her voice cut through his mental meanderings.

'It's okay.' No it wasn't, but he wasn't going to admit that. He was going to lie back in silence and not say anything smart or flirty or…anything.

'Won't be long.' Jessie watched as his eyelids flickered closed.

Then her gaze stretched the length of him. She swallowed hard and salvaged control of her jittery hormones.

No use. Her peripheral vision blurred into soft edges. Almost like the chlorine incident, but less painful. Kind of nice even. A buzzing in her ears gave her a dizzy sensation. The heat became stifling.

He must have felt it too. His eyes shot open. 'This is very cosy. You and me. Here.'

She fought for breath, concentrated on steadying her hand. *No conversation unless it's professionally based.* 'Don't get too comfortable. We have patients to see.'

'Why do you do that?'

'Duh? It's my job. Doctors see patients, it's kind of how it works.'

He groaned. 'No, why do you change the subject?'

'If I'm so transparent, why don't you tell me?'

She proffered the syringe, primed the needle. He'd hit the nail on the head. She did shut down every time he mentioned anything intimate. She had to. Self-protection. She couldn't give anything of herself to him. It would be too painful when it was time to leave.

'Okay, Luke, local anaesthetic first. Sharp sting. You know the drill.'

His hand tensed under hers. 'Okay, forget I mentioned anything. Go on, just stab me with the needle, you're the boss.'

'Well, I do have possession of all the sharp instruments. You, on the other hand, just have a gaping wound.'

'So?'

'So you have to play by my rules.'

'Which are?' His pupils flared, daring her.

Look, don't touch. 'Be a good boy. Stay quiet. Relax.'

He tilted his head and pierced her with his gaze. 'And you think I can relax with you so close?'

'It'll be over soon, then you can go.'

'Dammit, Jess, not until I've kissed you.'

'Luke!'

His words echoed off the stainless steel, rebounded off the clinical white walls, ground out loud and clear and tugged at her abdomen. He wanted to kiss her.

No.

'I'm going to pretend I didn't hear that. You're obviously still in shock. I have a job to do, Luke. Don't want you bleeding to death.'

'You're right. Of course. That would be messy.'

The needle hovering above his palm went out of focus.

Jessie cleared her throat, refocused and pressed the tip of the needle into his skin, concentrating hard on the wound, anything to avoid those startling grey eyes, his strong jaw, the angle of his chin. Those lips.

His hand twitched as she drew the needle back and injected again further along his palm. Any decent doctor would scan his face for signs of pain. But she couldn't bring herself to look for signs of anything. Knew only too well what she would see there.

She waited for the area to numb. Fiddled with the trolley. Resolutely refused to look at him.

His words hung thick in the air around them.

He wanted to kiss her.

And she wanted to kiss him right back.

A rush of heat and desire pooled in her abdomen. She tried to ignore it.

She couldn't kiss him. Wouldn't.

What good would it do? Except stoke a longing for something she couldn't have? She was leaving. *Leaving.* She couldn't kiss him.

She tied off the first suture. Began on the next. Held the soft smooth skin of his hand, imagined what pleasure his long fingers would create. Imagined them caressing her, holding her.

Still he said nothing.

She couldn't speak, her throat too loaded with thick need of him. The aroma of pure male lust mingling with the sharp tang of antiseptic made her feel crazy.

Concentrate.

Third suture. She tugged the end, aware he had shifted position. His breathing stuttered. If she moved her head an iota she'd be face to face with him. Within kissing distance.

He wanted to kiss her.

Fourth suture was finished before she knew it.

The fifth all tied off, a fresh dressing and bandage applied.

She was done. She breathed out heavily. Now she just needed to walk away. But the thought of kissing him lingered. Overwhelmed her. 'Okay, sutures out in a week.'

'Thanks.' He shuffled to the edge of his chair.

'For the record, I know what you're thinking now, too.'

'You do?' Heat flamed her cheeks.

He stood, his mouth close to her ear as he whispered, 'You want to kiss me too, but you're scared.'

'I'm not scared of anything.' *Liar. I'm scared of how you make me feel. Scared of this.*

'You want to kiss me, but you won't, not unless I make you.'

'I do not want to kiss you.' Her pulse jittered, her voice little more than a groan. 'And you can't *make* me.'

'I can and I will.' His hand touched her shoulder, his words a warm breeze on her skin. 'I dare you. I dare you to kiss me.'

'Right here? In the clinic? Are you mad?' She turned to face him, caught in the glare of his dangerous gaze, his eyes dark and filled with a need for her. Her legs almost buckled. Yes. *Yes,* she wanted to kiss him. Right here.

'Mad, crazy. Out of my skull, Jessica Price. Double dare. Kiss me.'

She giggled. 'Seriously, how old are you?'

'Thirty-two, but you make me feel like a teenager.' His smiling face grew serious. 'And I'm definitely old enough to know what I want.'

'Which is?' She forced the words out of her

closed throat, wanting and not wanting to hear what he had to say.

'You. Now. Here. I dare you. Just one. One kiss.'

She swallowed hard as warmth spread from his fingers to her shoulder, her nipples, her gut. Tingled up through her throat, her cheeks, until her body hummed with his heat.

She'd missed this. God knew, she'd tried to put cold distance between herself and anyone else. But she missed contact, touching, warmth.

She missed wanting and being wanted.

She missed kissing. She missed loving.

Most of all she missed loving.

Surely she deserved a small part of what everyone else in the world had? One small kiss wasn't a promise she couldn't keep. One small kiss couldn't hurt.

Besides, it was just a dare. Silly. Cute. Fun.

And if she was going to kiss anyone for a dare, it would definitely be Luke McKenzie.

Her heart thundered. She stared straight into those blazing eyes, took his face in her palms, pressed her lips gently against his mouth. 'I'm such a sucker for a dare.'

'I just knew you would be.' His mouth opened to hers, broadened into a smile.

He palmed the back of her neck and pulled her

closer, pressing his hard body against hers, his lips smooth and soft, wielding and wanting.

And still she couldn't stop herself smiling, grinning like an idiot as his hard heat pushed against her.

She'd done it. Taken something for herself. Made something beautiful. A simple kiss. To treasure.

Her teeth ground against his, making her pull away. She blinked up at him and laughed. 'Sorry. I just can't help smiling.'

'Do I have gloop on me or something?'

He checked his shirt, his black eyelashes grazing his cheek as he winked at her, his face alight with delight. Then he tipped his head back and laughed along with her. 'You're the strangest woman I have ever met.'

'Aw, shucks. Now you're making me blush.'

'And the most beguiling, and the most gorgeous.'

He swept a hand under her chin and tilted her head to his. 'Now, let's do this properly.'

'Another dare?'

'No. A necessity.'

'And then what?' She placed her shaking hands on his muscled chest, ready to push away if he said anything about happy ever after. She didn't want a promise or a commitment, something she couldn't return, but she wanted the taste of him, the smell of him, the strength of him around her. His heart pounded against her chest, her heartbeat raced in harmony, her body trembled.

He dipped his mouth close to hers. 'Then we'll run our clinic. And maybe do some more kissing.'

'Sounds like a plan.'

Her lips parted. His mouth brushed against hers, softly at first, then harder, hungry. His tongue slid in, hot, teasing, delicious.

Perfect.

CHAPTER EIGHT

WHAT on earth had he been thinking? Four days later Luke stood by his kitchen window, sipping coffee and contemplating the more kisses part of their deal.

So far they'd managed zip. Zilch. *Nada.* Zero.

Which was a good thing.

He inhaled the dark aroma and took a long drink.

Kissing her had been woefully foolish. Even more foolishly, he wanted to do it again.

How many times did he have to get involved with a drifter type before he learnt his lesson? For heaven's sake, did he have a death wish?

Thank God she'd turned down the invitation to Lucy's party. Whereas his daughter thought it nice to invite everyone she met, he was grateful for the distance he had forged. Four days post-kiss and they'd hardly managed a conversation. At least he could enjoy the festivities without worrying about what he said and how he said it. Or thinking about that kiss. Again.

A shrill blast of the doorbell heralded the end of the luxurious peace he'd been trying to steal before thirty-five children invaded his serenity. Peace? No such luck. There was definitely no peace when Jessie popped into his head.

He surveyed the balloon-infested house, added the finishing touches to his costume and answered the door. Armageddon had begun.

'Jessie? Wha...?' His breath caught somewhere in his chest. She stood in the doorway wearing a heavily embroidered brick-red, curve-hugging kimono-style dress that stopped just below her knees. Her hair was pinned back with what looked like chopsticks, a smear of shiny lipgloss covered her pout and jewelled jandals graced her feet. She had a teatowel-covered plate in one hand and the other draped casually and, oh, so sexily, against the doorjamb. 'I thought you weren't coming. I wasn't expecting you.'

'Clearly. Maggie said you needed a hand.' She glanced down at his bandaged palm. A small smile hovered on her lips. The plate she carried trembled slightly. 'Two hands. I could just leave this plate and go, if you prefer.'

'God, no. Can you imagine the grief I'd get if Lucy thought I hadn't asked you in?' The memory of that kiss shimmered between them like an invisible thread tugging and tightening. As it seemed to every time they shrugged past each other at work or in meetings. But neither of them mentioned it. 'She'll be thrilled you're here.'

Not as much as me. And probably not as confused either.

She stepped back, took in his pirate costume and raised an eyebrow. 'You really look the part, Cap'n Sparrow.'

'And you…well, amazing. I half expected you to come as some kind of ninja assassin.'

'I'm saving that for a grown-up party.' Her cheeks bloomed as red as her dress. 'This is something I picked up on my travels and the only thing I have that's remotely fancy enough for a dress-up party.'

She was smiling, but unease flashed across her eyes. He studied her again. There were genuine warm golden flecks in the startling blue, but she was guarded, keeping her distance. Friends still, then. Nothing more.

The kiss hadn't changed a thing. And yet it had changed everything. If the last few days were anything to go by, the friendly repartee they'd previously developed had dissolved into something akin to a nervous mumbling uncertainty.

She looked down at the plate in her hand. 'Better put this in the kitchen.'

'Sure. Come through.' Now she was in his house he didn't know how to act or what to say.

He'd always been in control of his emotions. He had no template for unbidden attraction. Maybe detached was the way to go.

She looked round the room. Pointing at the balloons, she laughed. 'You've been busy.'

'Yeah. And very soon my house and garden will be trashed, my nerves trodden on and my wallet lightened. Can't wait. Fun, fun, fun.'

'If you need a hand to clear up later, just ask.'

Later. He contemplated what could happen and his resolve threatened to wither. The sooner she left the house, the better. 'Maggie said she'd stay, and Becks too. We'll be fine. Thanks.'

'Don't say I didn't ask.' Relief tinged her words. She handed him the plate and removed the teatowel to reveal white sliced bread, spreadable butter and a bottle of hundreds and thousands. 'Here you are. My contribution to the healthy and nutritious party tea I know you'll have provided.'

'Actually, I got a caterer in.'

'I guessed you'd do something like that.' She frowned. 'Probably all sugar-free, fun-free snacks.

But no self-respecting three-year-old can party without fairy bread.'

'Fairy bread! Fairy bread!' Lucy ran into the lounge. 'Can I 'ave some?'

Luke's heart squeezed at her pretty pink dress and mop of curls. 'Can't believe she's three already. The years speed by so quickly. It seems like yesterday when we brought her home from Birthcare.'

'Before you know it she'll be a teenager. Lots of fun, fun, fun then.' Jessie grinned.

'Thanks for that.' He suddenly felt as if he was swimming in a shark-infested pool. 'The teenage years, danger at every turn.'

He would love his daughter without hesitation for the rest of his days but, judging by his own teenage experience, there was no hope in hell of understanding her once she turned thirteen. It was moments of panic like this when he wished her mother was still around to help. To share the lows and the highs.

Scratch that. Nothing made him wish Chloe would come home. Only Lucy was missing out on so much mother-daughter stuff.

'Don't you look gorgeous! Happy birthday, birthday girl.' Jess's gaze softened at his little girl as she straightened Lucy's lopsided sparkly wings. She might fight him with all guns blazing, but Jess sometimes had such a gentle way with her. 'Fairy bread for a fairy princess. But you'll have to wait. I have to make it first.'

'Can I help?' Lucy jumped up and down, grinning at the plate of delights. 'Ple-e-ease.'

'Of course you can.'

She'd make a great mother.

Whoa. *That is so not appropriate.*

Was he looking for a girlfriend or a replacement mother for Lucy?

Er….neither?

Get a grip, McKenzie. Jessie had grander things planned—Dunedin, international charity work. He couldn't ask her to give that up. Did he even want to? Hell, no. *Don't clip my wings*, Chloe had said more than once. Down the line Jessie would only resent them for holding her back. Just like Chloe had.

It was too much to contemplate. Where was his restraint? Where were those barriers he'd created?

Still clutching the plate in his good hand, he followed them through to the kitchen, listening to their excited chatter.

'Let's dry your hands on this towel.' Jess paused until the little girl had finished studiously wiping her hands, then pulled up a stool and lifted Lucy onto it. 'Now we need the ingredients. That means all the different things that make up the recipe.'

She glanced up at Luke, her eyebrows peaked and her eyes sparkled with laughter. He wanted to dive deep into them.

Instead, he placed the plate on the counter and turned to leave.

'Daddy? Where you going?'

'I have things to do, party girl.'

'Aw, Daddy.' Her lip puckered. Tantrum approaching? *Please, not today.*

Then she grinned. He felt the deep surge of love for his daughter. And knew he would give in to whatever she wanted. She'd wound him right round her finger. 'You got to help us.'

He sighed. 'Okay, little one. Just for a minute.'

He hovered in the background, away from temptation. From this vantage point he could watch how focused and gentle Jessie was with his daughter. She put one hundred per cent into everything she did, attacked every task with the same amount of verve and life and sense of fun. Unlike him. He stuck to rigid routine and order. Somehow he'd lost fun along the way.

'Right,' Jess continued, 'first we cut off the crusts. I'll do that with this sharp knife. We all know how dangerous sharp knives are, don't we, Daddy?'

'Sure.' He shrugged and held up his hook. 'Ver-r-ry messy it was too, young pipsqueak. So be careful.'

'Okay.' Lucy giggled. 'You're being silly.' Her face lit up as she listened and watched, completely bewitched by Jessica.

Was allowing her to get fond of Jess a mistake? He hoped not. He'd do anything to protect Lucy from heartache. Even if it meant creating more for himself.

He looked again at his *friend* in her impossibly tight dress, the gentle curve of her lips, the sensual arc of her neck. His chest constricted. The thought of her leaving already caused him enough pain.

'Daddy, look at me.' Lucy frowned and shook her head at him. 'I make fairy bread.'

'Aren't you lucky? Better clean your teeth extra well tonight.' He grimaced. 'And I'll know who to blame for the hyperactive kids.'

'Next we put the spread on. Then cut the bread into four little pieces. That's called quarters.' Jess put the knife down and glowered jokingly at Luke, that pout shimmering and mesmerising.

'And we both know all the research says that it's not the sugar that makes them hyperactive, it's the environment. It's a party, Luke. They'll have fun and get excited. That's kind of the point.'

She prodded his stomach with her forefinger. 'Lighten up, Cap'n Grump.'

Luke touched her hand, felt her fingers curl around his, squeeze gently then move away. Such a tender gesture that his heart didn't just lighten, it almost levitated out of his ribs. She smiled at him.

His daughter seemed so happy, the atmosphere in their house relaxed and warm. So like he'd imagined family life could be.

Family life, huh? He'd spent nine months tiptoeing around Chloe, careful to say and do the right thing in case she left. But she'd left anyway. Would Jessie be the same?

Right now she was like a fresh summer breeze blowing out the cobwebs of their cloistered lives, showing him how to enjoy parenthood instead of treating it as a task. Jess turned everything into fun. But would it still be fun after nine days, let alone nine months? Or would the restlessness set in? He couldn't take that risk again.

'Jess?' Lucy tugged at Jess's red hem.

'Okay, sweetheart. Now we press the spread side of the bread into the hundreds and thousands. Like this.' She poured the tiny multi-coloured candy threads onto a plate and pressed a piece of bread into it. Turned it upright. *'Voilà!* Fairy bread.'

'Villar!' echoed Lucy, as she copied Jess's flourish, then sank her teeth into a piece. 'Yummy.'

'Clever girl.' Luke kissed the top of Lucy's head, avoiding being eye-gouged by her tiara. 'Would you believe it? Bilingual at two.'

'Three!' Both females shouted at once.

He ducked as a teatowel flew past his head.

Luckily the doorbell chimed and saved him from the frothy avalanche of feminine giggles.

He grinned all the way to the front door. Lucy was having a great birthday. It couldn't get much better than this.

Then he paused with his hand on the doorhandle, remembering the other morning, seeing Jess rumpled and caught up in the sheets on his bed. Mmm, yes, it could.

A man could dream, couldn't he? Where was the harm in that? So long as he promised himself not to follow through.

'So, how's the slip, slop, slap station going?'

Luke's velvet voice made Jessie jump and remember why she needed to keep away from him. A few words from those lips made her legs wobble and her brain think about kissing him again.

A delicious idea, but totally against her self-isolation plan, which she'd executed to perfection over the last few days. Luckily he'd been so busy she hadn't had to work too hard at it.

So with her plan in motion and her heart at risk of being hijacked by Lucy, she'd declined the party invitation. She couldn't allow herself to be lured into this world. His world. Their world.

But then Maggie had milked the guilt by playing the poor-one-handed-daddy-who-needed-help card. And dropped casual comments about that 'sad motherless mite' until she'd worn Jessie down.

She sat at the sun-screening table and wiped her hands free of thick white gunk. Luckily, her preoccupation with UV factors had kept her out of his way. Until now. 'It's going pretty well, thanks. They've all slipped on something long-sleeved, slopped on sunscreen and slapped on their hats. We are sun smart and ready to go.'

'Amazing. Lucy usually puts up a fight when it comes to sun lotion.'

'Easy-peasy, sir.' She blinked up at Luke and saluted, choosing not to mention she'd bribed the kids with extra lollies if they did as they were told. She was getting the hang of this child-care thing. 'The sun won't have a chance of getting near their precious skin, Cap'n.'

'Great job. Thanks. Er...at ease.' He pulled up a small white plastic chair and sat next to her under the green-white striped gazebo. Then spent five minutes shifting uncomfortably as he tried to squeeze into the moulded plastic seat, until he eventually harrumphed, ripped off his wig and rubbed his head. 'I don't know, this having fun business is hard work.'

A laugh caught in her throat. The taut set of his jaw told her he was being serious. 'I think you're missing the point, Luke. It's not meant to be work. Relax. Look at Lucy, she's having a ball. Sure, it's crazy. But happy crazy.'

Luke stretched his legs out and looked like he truly was trying to relax. And failing.

'This is so out of my comfort zone at times. I was the ultimate carefree selfish med student, just ask Zac.' He shook his head as his pupils flared. 'We got into some trouble.'

'Yes, I got a whiff of some of it from Zac's emails years ago. How the heck he managed to balance study with such hilarity beats me.' Clearly parenthood had brought Luke hurtling back to earth with a bump. 'Lucy was a bit of a wake-up call, I expect?'

'Having a child is something else. Carefree's gone out the window. All I can think of is the potential danger. Falling off the bouncy castle, running too close to the barbecue, all this excitement setting off Lucy's asthma. I need to keep her safe.' He shrugged and his eyebrows rose in question. 'Overkill again?'

'No, it must always be at the back of your mind.'

'At the front usually. It's such a huge responsibility. There's so much I could get wrong and there's no one to bounce ideas off.'

'Hence spending a small fortune on those parenting books?' In response to his frown she explained, 'I saw them by the side of your bed. You could open your own library.'

He grimaced. 'Each one tells you something different. Time out. Controlled crying. The no-cry approach. It's a minefield.'

'Then don't read them all. Choose one and use the time you'd spend reading the rest to play with Lucy instead. She'll get a lot more out of it.' Jessie smiled at him squeezed so awkwardly into a tiny plastic seat, in his oversized leather waistcoat and clip-on dangly earring. Such an honourable man who just wanted to do the right thing, and nothing at all like an irresponsible, devil-may-care pirate.

She leant forward and touched his fake hook. Then patted his real hand, just so she could feel his warm skin under her fingers. 'You can only do so much to keep her safe. The rest you just have to leave to fate. Trust me on this, no matter what you do, you can't avoid the unavoidable.'

She left it at that. Spilling her guts about her sad life on this beautiful day would ruin the party, and her mood.

Jessie dragged his pirate wig on top of her bun and tried for a smile. 'Enjoy the time you have with her. You spend too much time worrying about making a perfect family and not enough time being one.'

He looked straight into her eyes, thought about it for a moment. The strain around his lips melted into a smile. 'You make it sound so easy. How did you get so wise?'

It certainly wasn't from experience. Her own childhood had been a sad blueprint on how not to rear a child, but instinct told her it had to be more about enjoyment and less about worry.

'It comes naturally. I got the brains and Zac got the beauty,' she joked.

'Oh, I don't know about that.' Luke tilted his head towards her and winked, making her insides wriggle a little. She was a sucker for his compliments. 'Zac's pretty clever too, you know.'

'Ha ha ha.'

'He tells me your parents were career geolo-

gists. Must have been interesting, all that travelling around.'

'Actually, it was as dull as dishwater, looking at
rocks instead of hanging out with other kids. All I
ever wanted was a standard-issue home, four solid
walls, friends to play with. Kind of like this.'

But even in adulthood the habit of moving had
stuck. Restlessness ate at her soul until she had to
pack and go. Certainly now there was no compul-
sion to contemplate a different kind of life.

'Zac also says he hasn't seen much of you.'

'We're not particularly close.' She felt a frown
developing. 'Did he ask you to talk to me about
this?'

'No. Why? Sore point?'

'Not really. I just wanted to see him. To catch up
after all this time.'

'He's a bit selfish at times, can't see past himself.
He's a decent bloke though. Underneath.'

But her disappointment was more about how
she'd let Zac down, not the other way round. She'd
wanted to tell him how much the accident had
affected her, to share some of her load, but had
had enough doleful pity from the hospital staff.
So she'd sent him away the one time he'd visited.

'My fault really. But his enthusiasm for a party
in Queenstown rather than a reunion with me feels

like a slap in my face.' But she probably deserved it. She'd acted pretty disgracefully. 'I guess there'll be other times.'

'It wasn't just the party, he really wanted to get there early for the sports med course. Honestly. I know how much he cares for you.'

She let that hang in the air and tested how it felt. Yes, her brother cared, and she cared for him too. But their unsettled childhood had left them both restless and disconnected.

Maybe it was maturity. Or loneliness. Maybe it was just the right time, but when he'd emailed to ask for her help she hadn't hesitated to say yes.

They peered into the glaring sun and the colourful chaos of the garden. Jessie recognised a few of the kids and their mums from the clinic. 'How many children did you invite?'

'Thirty-five.'

Her jaw dropped. 'That's one big social life for a three-year-old.'

'We invited the whole crèche. It seemed mean to leave anyone out. All up it's close to fifty, including you, the other parents, Becky and Maggie, of course.'

The older woman stood at the top of the garden incline, keeping order of a UV-protected Lycra-clad queue that had formed at the water slide—a thick black tarpaulin and a hose.

Becky monitored the bouncy castle currently bouncing a huddle of screeching fairies and princesses. Meanwhile, superheroes and cartoon characters fought imaginary foes with plastic swords as adults laughed, chided and chatted over a beer and a sandwich platter.

A kernel of childlike sparkle and froth percolated in Jessie's soul. All this laughter was infectious. 'Come on, Cap'n Grump, let's have some fun.'

She grabbed his ruffled shirtsleeve and dragged him to the face-painting stall.

'Turn him into a...hmm, a bear, please,' Jessie asked the off-duty crèche worker. She pushed Luke into the seat and held his hands over the back of the chair behind him, like a police officer cuffing an assailant.

'A bear?' He flinched as the first strokes of black covered his nose. 'In a pirate suit?'

'Stop wriggling.' She gave him an evil smile. 'Lucy will love it.'

She tipped her head back and laughed, then pushed him further into the seat. 'There's no escape. For some reason you remind me of a bear. All big and growly.'

And fiercely protective and warm, and would kill for those you love.

For a brief moment she imagined being wrapped in his bear hug. To feel his strength around her, anchoring her to this happy place. And felt the tight sting of sadness of something that could never be.

His face split into a grin, the tight furrows on his forehead smoothed and laughter lines etched his temples. 'Okay, okay. I'll take your advice. More fun, right? It'll wash off soon enough. Do your worst. You know, Jess, nothing you do ever seems to make sense.'

'Keep 'em guessing, I say.'

He rocked his chair back and craned his neck to scan her face. 'You can say that again.'

She held his wrists with one hand while she flicked through the book of face-paint characters available with the other. 'And then can you paint me as…oh, yes, I know. Can you do the Grinch? A smiley one. Got to turn this image around.'

'Well, if anyone can, it's you.' Luke's hand flailed around and caught her knee, squeezing and tickling, making her shriek and squirm and want to lean forward and cover his perfect laughing mouth with her own. To kiss him again, kiss and kiss some more.

'Yes, Jess, that would be just perfect.'

'Yes it would.' She smiled. 'Wouldn't it?'

But she wasn't thinking about face paint.

Having been cajoled into becoming the world's first pirate bear, Luke went to show the results to Lucy, which left Jessie free to fill her grumbling stomach.

As she made her way to the lunch table she watched him pick up his little girl and tickle her until she squealed. There was no denying that his love for Lucy was intense, but this afternoon there was a lightness to it too. She smiled. Maybe he was learning to relax a little. She hoped her wise words had had some impact.

Wise? Since when had it been wise to get so involved?

Maybe it was already too late.

Maybe she should cut her losses and leave now, while they were so distracted. Every second here reminded her of what she'd lost and, equally, cemented her resolve to keep on moving. She would put this little slip of emotional involvement down to experience and start Dunedin with a free conscience and a clean slate. She'd got over a lot worse, she could do it again.

A pale, thin woman Jessie recognised, but couldn't place, joined her at the huge feast.

'Hi. Dr Price, isn't it?'

No escape yet, then. Politeness deemed that she at least replied. Then left.

Jessie dragged her attention away from Luke while her brain scrambled to fit a name to the face. 'Yes, hello. Er…?'

'Stacey. Stacey Phillips.' The woman took a scoop of potato salad, looked longingly at the cold meat platter then added a spoonful of pesto pasta and veggies to her plate. 'I'm Kyle's mum. I came in to the clinic at the beginning of the week.'

'Sorry. Of course. I've seen so many new people this week my brain's a bit fuddled.'

Jessie looked at the selection of salads and drooled. Despite her misgivings, the uber-healthy food was delicious. 'How's Kyle doing?'

'The earache's gone now. He's right as rain. Thanks.'

'Cheese?' Jessie offered a double-cream Brie to the woman.

'No, thanks. I can't. Listeria and all that.'

Stacey glanced meaningfully at her stomach and the jigsaw pieces in Jessie's head slotted into place. The unwanted pregnancy. The reason she'd got to hold Luke's hand for the very first, and last, time.

'Oh, sorry. How's it going? Sickness abated yet?'

Stacey's voice lowered. 'No, still nibbling on the ginger biscuits morning and night.'

'It'll settle soon, hopefully.' She remembered Stacey as being around ten weeks. A lemon? Or was it a strawberry? 'Usually wears off by the end of the first trimester or so.'

They wandered to a quiet patch of Luke's quarter-acre garden. Bees and butterflies flitted amongst the lavender bushes, leaving a soft, comforting fragrance in their wake. An old rimu wood bench under an arbour of crimson bougainvillea seemed a good place to sit.

Jessie glanced towards Luke, who had taken control of the waterslide. Control being a loose term for utter shambles and bedlam.

As if he sensed her looking, he turned and waved. From this distance, thirty metres or so, she could feel his strength and warmth. She waved back and fleetingly wished that the other fifty-odd smiling people would melt away and leave just the two of them alone.

She looked back at Stacey. 'How are things going with your husband?'

'He's moved back in.'

'That's great. Is he pleased about the baby?'

'He still doesn't know.' Stacey moved food around her plate. 'I can't bring myself to tell him, and spoil things, when he's trying to make it work. We're trying. Apparently.'

'Trying?' Jessie swallowed a forkful of quinoa salad.

'To be nice. To get on. To make a future. Kyle's thrilled he's got his dad back home.'

Jessie looked at the woman's belly. There were no real signs yet, not unless she searched for the accentuated curve, but it would only be a matter of a few more weeks. 'And?'

'I'm trying to find the right time to tell him, hoping he'll soften.' Her lips tightened into a thin line. 'But I'm just going to mess up his plans.'

No different from her and Luke really. Staying in North Beach, even contemplating a future with him, meant messing up both of their lives. Big time. Jessie inhaled and blew out slowly. 'So how do you think he'll react when he finds out you're pregnant?'

The woman's eyes widened. 'He'll blow a fuse.'

'And the baby?' She almost daren't ask. *Love it. Please. Love it with all your heart. For always.*

Stacey put down her plate and ran a hand over her stomach. It was the first time Jessie had seen her do anything maternal towards her unborn child.

With a start she found herself mirroring the action. And then realised it was something she'd been doing a lot recently. Sheesh, why were all these deeply submerged emotions brimming to the surface again? She needed to control herself.

'I'll manage.' Stacey patted her belly. 'I read through those leaflets you gave me. Termination isn't an option. This baby…is the size of a lime already, can you imagine? It's real. I can't get rid of it.'

A lime. Of course. The citrus came first. She smiled. 'I totally understand.' *More than you can ever know.*

She understood Stacey's need to touch her growing belly, to relish the physical changes. She'd done it herself, watching in awe at how easily her body accommodated another living being. How she'd slipped into being *us*, not I. How eating for two became sleeping, walking, thinking for two. How much Michael had loved her body then.

And how things can change in an instant.

'Colin's a good man. He loves me but he worries about money.' Stacey sighed. 'He feels bad he can't give us all the things we want. But if he's dead set against another baby, then losing him is the price I'm going to have to pay.'

Jessie touched the woman's hand in a gesture of solidarity. 'I'm only here for another couple of weeks, but if there's anything I can do to help, please, just ask.'

'Are you not staying? The boys are nice and everything, but sometimes it's nice to see a lady doctor.'

Jessie looked out at the beautiful garden, the happy faces, Luke laughing and strolling lazily to the house with Maggie.

'I love it here, I do, but I need to move on. Like you said, sometimes we have to make sacrifices if we want to do the right thing.'

Knowing she wasn't making sense to anyone but herself, Jessie pretended to concentrate on her salad.

'Jess! Come…bouncy castle.' Lucy's shrill voice jerked her attention.

'I was thinking of going home, honey.'

The fairy-angel birthday girl trotted down the incline, breathless and pink-cheeked. Excitement fired in her eyes as she thrust her sticky hand onto Jessie's knee. 'Ple-e-ease.'

Then she coughed into her elbow.

'Good girl. Keep the bugs in a safe place, eh? Are you okay, Luce?' Jumping automatically into doctor mode Jessie did a quick scan of the girl's breathing. Fast, but not unduly so. She had just been careening round the garden after all. Her colour was good. No wheeze. She seemed fine.

'Yes. Bouncy castle. Please.'

'Sure your tummy and chest are okay?' Often kids this age slid into an asthma attack so quickly and their symptoms weren't always just respiratory. Many complained of stomachache too.

'Yes. Jess, c'mon.' The little girl tugged at Jessie's hand, and her bonny smile tugged at Jessie's heart-strings.

How could she possibly deny the cherub this? 'Okay, your wish is my command, princess. Perhaps we could have a blast on your inhaler on the way. I don't like the sound of your cough.'

'Jessie-ee.' The little madam rolled her eyes and put her hands on her hips in the style of a sixteen-year-old diva. Jessie squirmed at the glimpse of attitude. Growing up way too fast. Luke had an interesting time ahead. 'Come on.'

'Inhaler first.'

She felt the shudder of excitement as Lucy grabbed her hand. Looking over at the monstrous cartoon castle bobbing in the wind, Jessie began to regret saying yes already. She stood and smiled at Stacey. 'Wish me luck.'

CHAPTER NINE

A BIT like motion sickness mixed with being drunk. Or possibly walking on the moon, Jessie mused as she tried to keep her limbs and thoughts coherent.

A blur of pink shrieking streaks surrounded her as she tumbled hither and thither in her very restrictive kimono.

'Ring-a-ring of roses…' They had her holding hands in a circle now, wide smiles all round as they atishooed and fell down. Bounced up. And down. Up again.

The hardest part was keeping her modesty. Bouncy castles were so not her thing.

This was not necessarily the best time to discover this.

'Having fun?' Luke shouted from the safety of terra firma. At least she thought it was him, but her vision had begun to blur with nausea. All she had to go on was the warm velvet voice that stroked her deep inside. Yes, definitely him.

'Yes… Ouch!' Her mouth collided with a three-year-old's skull. Jessie's head snapped back and she rolled backwards, clutching her face. A sharp pain stung her lip and the world tipped even more sideways as shimmery stars floated across her vision.

She blinked. Two blurry Lukes stared back at her from the garden. Two. She kind of liked that idea. Yummy. Twice the fun.

Double the trouble.

She tried to reorientate herself, to stand up from the all-fours position she found herself in. But it was almost impossible as she reeled back and forth.

The skull she'd knocked against seemed unharmed. The little girl, one of the party princesses, rubbed her head a bit, laughed and carried on jumping.

How Jessie wished she was young again.

'Hey, you okay?' Luke was on the castle, lolloping towards her. His smiling bear face was filled with genuine concern, long limbs windmilling as he tried to hurry over the wobbling PVC floor.

'I'm fine.' She sounded like she was speaking through a mouthful of cotton wool. A metallic taste tanged in her mouth. Her lip pulsed with a dull ache and she dabbed it gingerly. 'At least I thought I was fine. I'm bleeding.'

'That looks nasty.' Kneeling in front of her, he

ran his thumb gently across her lip. Desire shivered through her body, reaching every part of her. His serious eyes gazed down, the connection between them a growing living thing, no matter how much they tried to pretend otherwise. No matter how much distance they forged. 'You want me to kiss it better?'

'Luke!' A shot of heat fired into her gut, and her cheeks. His mouth was so close all she had to do was inch up. A few tiny millimetres, a heartbeat, and then she could cover his mouth with hers. She scanned the garden. Yes, still heaving with onlookers. 'In front of all these people?'

'Hey, I kiss Lucy's scrapes all the time. Why should you get different treatment?'

She smiled, the tightness of her lip making her wince. 'I think we should get off here and behave like responsible grown-ups.'

'Okay, but only if you give me a rain-check.'

'Like never?' Any kissing would happen behind closed doors.

It wasn't a question of if but when. At what point did kissing him become inevitable? And then what?

Nothing. She couldn't risk him seeing her scars, the look on his face when he saw them. Another rejection.

'Steady, there.' A sudden pitch had him wrapping his arms tightly round her. His taut body slammed against her, filling her with undeniable hot need. 'Nice and close, Dr Price.'

'Er...we still have an audience.'

'Just saving a damsel in distress. I could pretend I'm giving you the kiss of life. Okay, stop frowning; I'm joking.'

In one swift move he had her in his arms and was striding off the wretched castle. He held her tight to his hard chest, his heart beating wildly with every step. She pressed her cheek to his ribcage and relished his heat.

He smiled down at her, wickedness glinting in his eyes. 'You don't think they suspect already? Maggie's been singing the wedding march almost since the day you arrived.'

She groaned. 'I know. I haven't been blind to her matchmaking efforts.' *Like making me come to this party in the first place.* 'She needs a different focus in life.'

'Twenty years of wedded bliss, she just wants me to have the same.'

Gently placing her on a bench, he bent and examined her lip more closely. His breath whispered over her skin. She closed her eyes and let his fingertips massage a soft trail down her cheek, over her lip. Awareness hummed through her as she remembered how he tasted, how his fingers had caressed her skin. How her body tingled and an ache fizzed in her veins.

His voice broke into her thoughts, adding extra layers of dangerous whisky-warm deliciousness. 'Just wait here, I'll get some ice.'

'Good idea.' Ice, yes, ice would douse this need. She opened her eyes to see him looking at her curiously, then he shook his head quickly, as if trying to swipe his thoughts away. A wry smile hovered on his lips. Maybe he'd been remembering their kiss too.

Over his shoulder she caught sight of Lucy standing alone by the waterslide. Her screwed-up face was pale, and her shoulders shifted up and down incessantly. From this distance she looked like she was trying to breathe underwater, grasping, gulping at the air.

The heat in Jessie's gut flowed ice-cold. 'Luke! Quick, Lucy's in trouble.'

Luke's smile dissolved and his features turned to granite. Within a second he had whipped Lucy from the waterslide and was striding up the garden and into the house.

Jessie raced after them as fast as a tight kimono

would allow, back up the incline, past the skipping, sliding zoo of kids. She found them in the kitchen.

'What do you need?'

'Keep her calm.' Stony-faced, Luke flicked a switch and a nebuliser whirred into action. 'She hates this.'

'No wonder.' The medicine designed to make her better steamed out through a mask that almost covered her entire face. 'For a wee toddler trying to breathe, placing something over her mouth probably seems really dumb.'

Lucy pulled at the elastic holding the mask in place. 'No. No. No.'

'Hey, Lucy. Come here. Come to Jessie.' Jessie's heart pinched as she lifted the little girl onto her lap. Some deep instinct seemed to take over and she glimpsed what it might be like to be a parent. It wasn't just about love. Worry and confusion and affection meshed inside her.

The child wriggled to tug at the mask again, a pale sweaty sheen on her forehead. She arched her back against Jessie's ribs and pushed her chest out. 'No.'

Luke repositioned the mask, took Lucy's pulse and counted her resps. 'Way too fast. Keep still, Lucy. This is Daddy's magic medicine. It always makes you feel better, eh?'

His actions were systematic and regimented. Nebuliser. Mask. Pulse. Resp rate. No emotion flickered. He was well and truly in charge of this emergency. Jessie got the feeling it happened often and he was well practised. But what the hell was going on his head? Watching your daughter's lips turn pale blue as she struggled for breath must pierce to the core. It certainly stabbed Jessie somewhere deep in her soul.

The poor tot's accessory muscles in her chest and neck were working overtime. Her abdomen hollowed deeply with every gasp. Soon she'd be exhausted.

And that would be the time to call the ambulance. Jessie prayed things wouldn't get that severe. She couldn't bear the thought of seeing Lucy dancing and singing one minute and hooked up to machines almost in the next difficult breath. Asthma could kill, she knew that well enough. They needed her…Jessie *needed* her…to get this medicine deep into her constricted lungs. 'I gave her some puffs on her inhaler not an hour ago. She seemed fine then.'

'These things come on so quickly. They can also get fixed really quickly too. She'll be fine, if she could stop fighting it.'

Her mind roiling for a solution, Jessie grasped

at the first thing she thought of that might make a
difference to Lucy.

'There was a man lived in the moon, in the moon,
in the moon...' She couldn't believe she was actually singing. But anything was worth a shot. She
rocked slowly from side to side, holding the mask
over Lucy's face with one hand and stroking the
little girl's hair with her other. Singing quietly into
her ear.

'There was a man lived in the moon, and his
name was Aikendrum.'

'Jess?' Lucy's head rubbed against Jessie's chest
as she stared up into Jessie's face. For a second the
kid stilled. Then she tried to push the mask up onto
her forehead. 'No like it.'

But for a moment there, she'd been transfixed.
If only she could be distracted for long enough...

'And his hair was made of spaghetti, spaghetti...'
Jessie's voice got louder. She played with the pirate
wig, long tendrils of dreadlocks that just happened
to hang like thin pieces of pasta. Tickled Lucy's
face with the braids. 'Spaghetti.'

Lucy stopped wriggling, pulled at the wig. And
took a deep breath of the nebulised air. ''Getti?'

'Yuk! Spaghetti hair.' Jessie watched her take
another breath, and then another, seemingly forgetting the panic and the fear.

Feeling Lucy's pulse, Luke nodded. 'Great one. Keep going, babe.'

Was he talking to her or Lucy? Jessie didn't know or care. Her focus was solely on keeping the mask over the snub nose and mouth, getting this magic mist into the tiny branches of her airways. 'And his eyes were made out of meatballs… meatballs…'

In her arms she felt a little shiver. Lucy had giggled. Jessie's heart soared. 'Either the nebulised Ventolin has started to work, or my terrible singing has stunned her into submission.'

'Her breathing's slowing to a better rate.' He checked Lucy's lips. 'Pinked up a bit now too.'

'And his nose was made of cheese…cheese… cheese.' Careful to whisper as calm descended. Lucy sat quietly as the nebuliser hissed and buzzed the last of its medicine into the mask.

'Have a little rest now.' Jessie took one of Lucy's tiny fists and threaded a finger into it. She stroked the cool skin, noticed the tiny crescents on her fingernails. Pink and perfect.

How amazing she was.

Lucy's eyes flickered open. 'Funny Jess.' Then they closed again as she curled her hand into Jessie's, so trusting. So accepting.

'You really have a knack with her.' Luke bent

and stroked the soft down of Lucy's cheek, his expression softening around his daughter. 'But that tune's going to bug me for the rest of the day.'

'Don't even know where I dredged it up from. My dad used to sing it to me, I think. Or maybe it was just some song on the radio.'

Resting his hands against the kitchen bench, Luke inhaled deeply, lost in thought. His shoulders were rigid, his jaw muscle twitching.

'You okay?' Jessie had to whisper so as not to wake Lucy, who lolled heavily on her lap. 'Tough break, eh?'

'Yeah. And it's not finished yet. My guess is that she'll need regular nebs for the next day or so.'

He turned to face Jess and ran a hand over his forehead. Despite his happy bear face paint, he looked down, jaded and scared. Time to allow the emotion to flow. It was the way of things for a medic. And, it would appear, for a parent. Act first, feel later. 'I hate seeing her like that. Thanks for everything, Jess. It really helped, having you here.'

'I didn't do anything really. She just needed distracting.'

'When she's like this I jump into doctor mode. Got to get her better. I know she's scared, but I have to use any means necessary to get those drugs into her. I've never tried singing before.' He laughed. 'But with my toneless voice, I think I'll leave it.'

'It must be hard, coping on your own. You must miss Chloe at times like this.'

'I don't miss her at all.' The fear was replaced with ill-disguised anger. 'Lucy wasn't diagnosed until way after Chloe had left. She's never had to watch her daughter suffer.'

Her heart went out to him. 'You do great.'

'I do enough. Being a solo parent can be difficult. Sometimes you just need two pairs of hands. Like just then. Someone to hold her, someone to give her the neb.'

He glanced at the sleeping child and lowered his voice. 'I'm all about keeping her safe and well. But you're right, we do need more fun. And I'm no good at the touchy-feely things. Seeing her play with your hair, the way she looks at you, responds to your gentleness, makes me realise what she needs. And sometimes it's more than I have. Thank God there was just one kid in all this mess. Chloe got out just in time.'

'You were planning more?'

'Yes. In hindsight it would have been a really s tupid idea. But we talked about it.' He removed the mask from Lucy's face, lifted her from Jessie's drooping arms and tiptoed into the lounge. Together they laid her on the sofa and covered her with a pale cream mohair throw. Even asleep she coughed as if trying to squeeze as much air into her lungs as she could.

Luke hunched on the floor against the sofa, Jessie crouched next to him. Almost touching him, wanting to but lacking the guts. Being around them both had become so natural, but taking it to the next level—easy intimacy—was something she didn't know if she could do.

'I never planned for Lucy to be an only child.' He glanced over at the sleeping child. 'There was just me growing up and I hated it. I always wanted a whole clan of kids.'

Of course he would. Few men didn't want to extend their lineage, they were hard-wired to do it, but hearing him say it hurt more than she'd imagined.

Glad she hadn't reached out to him, she wrapped her hands around her knees. 'Well, if Maggie has her way, you'll be living a life of wedded bliss in no time.'

'You offering?' His eyes sparked jokey interest.

She nearly choked. 'It was a figure of speech. Just saying, the way she clucks around you.'

'Even Zac's at it. Got it into his head that I need a good woman.' He grimaced. 'Two disastrous blind dates taught me never to trust your brother's taste in women.'

A tight rap at the door had them both turning round.

Stacey stood in the doorway, clutching Kyle's hand. 'Is Lucy okay?'

'She's fine now, thanks. But she's flat out for the count.' Luke gave a relieved smile. 'How's the party? Still in full swing?'

Stacey looked down with kind eyes at the sleeping babe. 'Everyone's gone. We just came to say goodbye and thank you for having us. Maggie says she's tidied up and taken a few of the kids home.'

'Thanks, Stacey. Hope Lucy's attack didn't spoil everyone's fun.'

'We had a great time.' She turned to Jessie and laughed. 'With all this drama I guess you definitely won't be wanting to stay? You'll go and look for a quieter life somewhere else.'

Luke's eyebrows rose, his eyes brightened. 'You thinking about staying, Jess?'

'We talked about it, that's all.' Jessie looked up into his face and for a moment was lost.

Change the subject. Because if you ask I just might say yes. She dragged her gaze away, gathered a few empty beakers from the coffee table.

'Guess we should get this place sorted. And I'll show you out, Stacey.'

As the last of the guests left Lucy let out a whimpering cry. Jessie was by the little girl's side in an instant. 'You feeling okay, baby?'

Baby. Amazing that a single word could tear her heart to pieces.

'Where's cake? Birthday cake?'

The cake, the 'Happy birthday to you'. All forgotten in the midst of the emergency. 'Oh, sweetie, everyone's gone home.'

The little face crumpled. Jessie found herself scrabbling around, trying to make things better. What could take the place of a host of adoring smiley faces and birthday cake, being the birthday princess, the centre of attention?

'How about when you're feeling up to it, we go out for a trip somewhere? Maybe the aquarium, or...I know...the Magic Planet. We could look at the Man in the Moon by telescope.'

'Yes, please!' A tired blurry smile transformed Lucy's face. 'Now? Can we go now?'

'Sounds like a great idea.' Luke's voice boomed above them. 'Soon, but not today. Your breathing's still poorly, you need to stay quiet for a few days.'

Jessie's gaze travelled the length of him, settling on his face. A soothing calm descended on her.

Just looking at him made her feel good. How on earth had it got to this?

'And right now it's time for bed, missy.' He swooped the little girl into his arms and nodded at Jessie. 'See you in a few minutes?'

'I'll tidy up a bit.' After all, what was the hurry to leave? Staying here might be risky and foolish. But it was a darned sight better than going home to an empty house.

She started to gather the balloons into a huge rainbow bouquet, but keeping busy didn't erase the memory of how interested Luke had looked when she'd mentioned staying in North Beach. Somewhere along the line, she sensed, he'd got as involved as she had.

The temptation to stay was getting greater every day, even though she knew it was foolhardy. *Especially* now she knew of Luke's intention to fill his house with baby McKenzies.

Knowing she couldn't give Luke what he wanted, and deserved, made her feel wretched. There was also Lucy to consider; Jess shouldn't get involved with this tiny mite who had already been abandoned by one woman. And yet keeping away from them was becoming as impossible as staying would be.

Cold crept under her skin as she watched him

carry Lucy out of the room. When she left she might bruise his heart a little. But what would she do to her own?

Luke found Jessie in the lounge knee deep in balloons and presents. As always, his breathing did its funny excited jiggly thing when he saw her. If he didn't get a hold on it soon, he'd need Lucy's inhaler just to survive an hour in Jess's company.

Now he was alone with her, he didn't know what to say.

How about 'Thanks, you want to stay the night?' Or 'Thanks, and goodnight'?

Whichever, he needed to clear the air. He couldn't function with this unfulfilled desire zapping around them. He handed her a glass of chilled pinot gris and watched as she ran its cool bowl over her swollen mouth. Lucky glass.

She took a sip. Her slender throat moved delicately, so creamy white compared to the lurid green face paint. She placed the wine glass on the windowsill and folded wrapping paper into the recycling bin. 'She went off to sleep okay?'

'Like a light. Barely had the energy to use her spacer.' He crumpled up the rest of the wrapping mountain and stuffed it into the bin. Then switched on the baby listener. 'Haven't used it in ages. Useful for times like this. Shame, she was having a great time until the asthma attack.'

'Me too.' Jess gave him a lopsided, kooky grin. 'Shame you washed your face paint off. I kind of liked you all growly.'

'I was glad to be rid of it. Too itchy.' He ran a hand to his jaw while his heart did a little jig. She liked him growly. It was a start. 'How's the lip?'

'Sore. Still, there's a silver lining. I've got a trout pout. People pay hundreds of dollars to look like this.' She preened her hair and threw him a theatrical kiss. '*Dahling*. Although it's more like a one-sided reaction to a dodgy filler.'

But still very kissable. 'Okay. Come with me.'

'Wha—?'

He took her hand before she could argue, stood her by the kitchen sink. 'Déjà vu. In the kitchen, just like our first meeting.'

'But this time my face is green, not my hair. So... what are you going to do with me?'

She laughed, but the smile stopped before it reached her eyes. The only emotions Luke could read there were a mix of desire and fear. Desire he could definitely deal with. But visceral fear? Fear of what? Him? Being hurt? That husband had broken her heart, he was sure of it. Something was blocking her willingness to get close. Hell, he was one to talk. What a pair.

Not a pair—yet.

Tread carefully. If he pushed too hard she'd probably close down completely.

'I'm going to do what we should have done a while ago.' He smiled at the flash of anxiety. 'Put ice on it.'

He trapped her against the sink, dampened a flannel and wiped the green face paint away. 'That's better. I can see you properly now. You are so beautiful, you know.'

She opened her mouth to speak then seemed to change her mind. Just looked at him with a strange expression, scrutinising him.

He couldn't drag his eyes away from hers. She was beautiful. Really beautiful. And, for all her bravado, surprisingly fragile.

He reached into the freezer, placed a bag of frozen peas against her lip. 'There, we'll soon have you back to normal.'

'Thanks.' She laughed. 'Whatever *normal* is. You're so kind.'

Huge soft blue eyes stared up at him. There was something in there he hadn't seen before. A flicker of trust?

That was a big thing for her. And for him.

'I can't help it. You make me crazy.' He leaned closer.

He ran his thumb along her cheek, stroked the soft down of her skin. Tried hard not to think about her sensual eyes staring up at him, her full swollen lips.

And failed. 'Now, about those kisses you promised.'

Resting the bag of peas on the drainer, she shook her head again. 'No, Luke, we agreed, remember? Friends only.'

'You're right.' He stepped away. 'Absolutely. I'm sorry. I shouldn't…'

'No.' Jessie took a shallow breath. Then another. Grabbed his wrist as he turned from her. *What the hell?*

No matter how much her head said she shouldn't do this, her body ached for it. Maybe to…get him out of her system. A brief kiss then she'd be satiated.

Would she? One kiss could lead to more, and more, and then inevitably he'd see her scars. Then the kiss would definitely end. And any hope. She needed to leave. Now, before it was too late.

But he tipped his head, inches away from her mouth. He smelt of soap and cinnamon, an intoxicating mix. He glanced at her fingers clasping his arm. Smiled. Ran his thumb over her bruised lip. 'I'll be gentle.'

The look he gave her was a question, a promise. Another dare. How could she resist?

'Gentle? Don't even think about it,' she groaned, lost in her need for him.

Her arms curled around his neck. She blinked up at him, her tongue slicked a line along her lips, her breathing came in little gasps as she pulled him closer and found his mouth with hers.

Her lips were ice-cold and she tasted of honeyed wine. He wanted to drink her in, every beautiful drop. Very gently he traced butterfly kisses around her luscious mouth, slowly kissing along the line of bruising.

It wasn't enough. He wanted more of her.

To hell with treading carefully—he wanted to rush in and capture the whole deal. He wanted Jess and her crazy whirlwind of fun and fragility. He wanted her in his bed, by his side. He wanted her unlike anything he'd ever wanted before.

He inhaled her flowery scent, drunk on the heady aroma.

What did he want? For her to stay? That was so far off both their radars. But right now it seemed possible. He couldn't think straight with her here.

He wanted this. Her smell, her soft body in his arms. This kiss.

Yes, that's what he wanted. More than that and he was lost.

'Jess,' he murmured as he unpinned her hair. It fell in tendrils around her shoulders and he buried his hands in her blonde curls as he kissed her, suffusing her lips with his heat.

She deepened the kiss further, sliding her tongue into his mouth, filling him with spasms of heat and desire. Her tight body pressed against his; beneath her dress he felt the swell of her breasts, the curve of her hips, and was lost with the power of his need for her.

Her breathing staccatoed as she pulled away a little. 'God, this is so good.'

'So why did we stop?' She was right, of course. They should stop. But she tasted so good, felt so right in his arms, so damned good he couldn't stop. He grasped her tiny waist, ran his hands down her belly.

She gasped, edged sideways, moved his hands to her back. He cupped her bottom and pulled her closer. Lust filled her gaze. 'I vowed I'd keep my distance.'

'And how's that panning out for you?' he murmured.

'Mmm. Needs a little work.'

He unbuttoned the first corded coil at her neck and kissed her pale, soft skin, felt her muscles tense, and then she wriggled closer.

In one swift move he hitched her onto the drainer, the kimono riding up her sweet, pale thighs. He swallowed hard, struggling with the urgent need to slide deep inside her right there.

She curled her legs around his waist and drew him nearer. 'We really should stop,' she groaned between kisses, then she nuzzled her head against his forehead and chewed the unswollen corner of her lip.

When their breathing slowed and they finally came up for air he was frowning.

'Did I do something wrong?' Jessie asked, her heart slamming in her chest. She'd been so crazy for him she hadn't been able to think straight. Now, though, the edges of everything were blurred. She didn't know which way was up. But seeing Luke's frown, she was pretty sure things were headed in a downward spiral.

'No. You did everything right. You kiss like a goddess, and I don't want it to stop. But we need to talk.'

No. Please. Could he feel her scars through her dress? Had he guessed when she'd moved his hands away from her stomach? She rested her head against his chest, felt the raging strength of his heartbeat, achingly aware of his hardness between them. So full of life and heat and desire.

For her. No, he hadn't guessed. He still wanted her.

She was both frightened and excited at the same time. 'Do we have to talk?'

He nodded. 'This is a fine time to discover I have principles. Believe me, I'm more sorry than you are.' He looked down at his groin. 'Sorry mate.'

'You're speaking to your tackle? That's novel.'

'It has a mind of its own. And wants to lead the way, but I'm struggling here.' He teased a curl of her hair and rubbed it through his fingers. He swallowed a large mouthful of the honey-coloured liquid. She sensed it was Dutch courage. 'I want you like crazy but I know you're holding back.'

'Please, Luke. No.' She knew what was coming. And she couldn't blame him, she'd been giving him mixed signals and he deserved an honest explanation. She wanted him so much, but wanting wouldn't get her anywhere. Except into trouble.

Suddenly running seemed a good option, to escape the intensity of his gaze. His large frame filled the tiny kitchen space. His questions probed at something she'd hidden deep inside. She wasn't ready to tell him her story yet, if ever, but there was no escaping this. If only she was as brave and as wise as he believed her to be.

'I'm not good at relationships.'

That wasn't a lie. After the accident she'd been terrible to Michael, and he'd been terrible back. So much guilt and blame had fuelled their arguments, they hadn't even been able to get past a conciliatory 'Hello' without unleashing a tirade of insults. 'I'm better off not getting involved.'

Luke took the stack of plastic plates she handed him and wiped them one by one. His head tipped towards her, his voice very gentle, very understanding. He looked at her with compassion and fading vestiges of the passion they'd just shared.

'Maybe you haven't met the right guy. Until now.'

If ever there was a right guy, it would be him. Only there could be no right guy. She felt like a rat. Worse than a rat. 'Maybe.'

'I'm not imagining this, Jess. It's hot, it's intense. It's real, isn't it?'

'Yes. It is. It's real.' She gulped another mouthful of wine. She couldn't deny him. 'But it can't go anywhere, you said it yourself. I'm heading to Dunedin in a few days. After that, who knows?'

Let me fly, Luke.

'You're right. I know. Your life isn't here. You're

on your way to bigger and better things. Just wish-ful thinking on my part.'

Luke took a step away from her and her entic-ing scent. Her crazy curls and delicious mouth. His head was spinning with lust and confusion. Thank God he hadn't got in too deep. Hadn't asked her to stay. Made too much of a fool of himself. Again. But, damn, he wanted her so much his heart ached. 'A reality check is probably a good thing. Bad tim-ing, huh?'

'You could say that. Maybe in another lifetime.'

'I'm hardly a good catch anyway, a single dad with a fractious toddler.'

'Any woman would be lucky to have you. Chloe must be out of her mind...'

The baby listener crackled. A wheezy cough drifted through the speaker amplified in stereo by the sounds of Lucy's struggles coming from upstairs. He gave her a half-hearted smile. 'Don't know why I bother with the listener really, I can hear her perfectly well without it.'

'You'd better go to her.'

'I know. She needs me.'

She followed him to the hallway. His finger-tips tangled in her hair as he planted a chaste kiss on her cheek. The wild need still zinged between them. A scary energy, he realised, that neither knew how to harness. Bad timing indeed.

Stay. The word was almost out of Luke's mouth before he could stop it. He clamped his lips shut.

It was a wild thought. He wasn't even sure if he meant just a few minutes, just tonight or for ever.

But he couldn't ask her. Not after what had just happened. Any conversation about staying would have to come from her. She'd have to want to stay, and right now she seemed hellbent on leaving.

CHAPTER TEN

SEVEN nights left.

Seven nights until that flight to Dunedin.

It ticked in Jessie's head like a metronome, faster and faster.

As the week drew to a close the thought of leaving Luke and Lucy filled her with dread. Like their stolen kisses, her imminent departure was never mentioned but it hung in the air around them, tainted their conversations with regret for what could have been, in another lifetime.

Her days were spent at work, covering for Luke as he took time off to look after Lucy.

Her nights were spent alone, tossing and turning under a flimsy sheet, fighting the stifling humidity and her almost uncontrollable desire to stalk over to his house, climb into his bed and make love to him. Being so close and yet not close almost drove her insane.

By Saturday Lucy had recovered enough to undertake their promised trip.

'Are you sure she's warm enough?' Jessie examined Lucy's pale arms sticking out of the buggy she'd insisted they take just in case the little girl tired. 'Has she had her Ventolin?'

Grinning at her as he pushed the stroller through the Magic Planet automatic doors, Luke shook his head. 'You're worse than me. She's fine. Look at her.'

Her eyes the size of the moon itself, Lucy's grin split her face. She shucked out of her buggy and crossed the threshold into the strange starry world of the universe.

'I wasn't sure about coming here, to be honest. I didn't think three-year-olds would be interested in this kind of stuff,' Jessie breathlessly said to Luke as she tried to keep up with them dashing between exhibits. Every time they stopped to read a poster or an information panel Lucy grabbed his hand and moved them along.

'You obviously hadn't reckoned on her insatiable appetite for fun. Hey, let's have a photo of my girls next to that replica NASA suit.'

'Your girls?' Jess looked at him with a mix of interest and curiosity. She laughed as she posed. 'Dr Territorial!'

His girls. It was what he used to call his family—Chloe and Lucy.

It had just slipped out. From nowhere. From the bright hope in his chest as he watched Jessie with his daughter. The last couple of weeks had felt more like family than anything he'd ever experienced with Chloe.

The thought of his ex made him shudder. He should take heed of his experience with her. He'd put trust and faith into his marriage, but she'd broken his heart, and his daughter's. It had taken two years to get her out of his system. Years marked by Lucy's milestones imprinted on his heart like tender bruises.

'Excuse me.' A young girl, in her early twenties, wearing a tight singlet and with a camera hanging from her neck, approached them. 'Would y'all mind taking a photo of us?'

A group of six American Beauties beamed at him, yattering about the quaintness of the country, the heat in February, the cute kid in the stroller.

'Sure.' Luke snapped a few pictures on their digital camera. They gathered like bees around a pot to check his framing and focus.

There's nothing wrong with my focus, he thought as he watched Jess smiling and chatting to the group. At least, what filled his vision was crystal clear. A beautiful woman and a darling girl. *His girls.*

All week he'd missed Jessie during the day, counted the long hours until her cheery face appeared after dinner for an hour to check up on Lucy.

And each time she'd visited he'd ached to touch her. A deep raging need that had threatened to overpower him. But then Lucy had got in the way, and it just hadn't been the right time.

Damn it, he was scared. Scared to ask her to stay. Scared to push things to some place she didn't want to go.

Scared he'd get broken all over again when she left.

'Why, thank you, that's just great.' The girl flashed him a perfect smile with her perfect white teeth. A glint in her eye told him she could be interested. And once, long ago, he might have been too. 'What a beautiful daughter, sir. She's got your looks.'

She glanced over at Jess, who suddenly slid her arm into his and rested her head on his shoulder. *He's mine*, her actions said. 'I guess she's got your smile, too, Mom. What a neat family.'

Her eyes flaring with something he could only describe as alarm, Jess tensed. A rash of red crept up her neck. 'Er…I'm not…I mean… Thanks.'

'Are you my mummy, Jess?' Lucy grinned up

at her. Light flickered in her innocent eyes as excitement seemed to overpower her tiredness. He'd never seen his daughter look like she wanted anything more. 'Plee-ease.'

Oh, God. His stomach tightened into a knotty fist. What to do? Jess looked at him and shook her head. This was what he'd wanted to avoid, that his daughter would get too attached. And then abandoned again.

He knelt at the buggy and quickly prepared his usual speech about Chloe. About how Lucy's mother was far away but that he was sure she always thought about her little girl. Tried to keep the anger out of his voice.

He opened his mouth to speak but Jessie interrupted, 'No, silly.' She tickled Lucy and smiled at her gently. Something akin to a mother's love, or at least real deep affection emanated from her eyes. 'You already have a mummy. I'm the Grinch, remember?'

'Silly Jess.' Lucy nodded. 'You're not mean. You're nice.'

'And so. Are. You.'

Lucy squealed in delight at Jessie's tickles.

Jess laughed too, her face soft and warm. Did she understand the effect she had on everyone?

How much she lit up Lucy's world? How could she leave? He just didn't get it.

'I'm not your mummy, I can't ever be that because mums are very special and we only have one of them. But I'm your friend. Always.'

Jess stroked Lucy's hair then curled her pinkie into the little girl's chubby fingers and shook it. A more tender gesture than he'd ever seen Chloe make towards her daughter. A bitter-sweet weight crushed his chest. How he wished things had been different. How he wished Chloe hadn't tarnished his ability to trust. And that Jess had different plans for her life.

'Wherever you are you can always peer up at the night sky and know we're looking at the same moon. Say, "Hi Jess!" And if you ever need me, I'll be there.' Jess stood up and smiled. 'I'm starting to sound like my father. Making hollow promises. Bad idea. Okay, so where's the ice cream?'

Luke followed her to the counter. It wasn't until he turned to ask her favourite flavour that he noticed the trace of a tear. 'Thanks for that.' He squeezed her against him, enjoying the weight of her pressed close but unsure whether to mention what had just happened. 'You know, that woman was just being nice.'

'I know.' Her shoulders straightened and she

grinned. Wiped her face with the back of her hand. Feisty Jess was back. 'And she fancied you.'

So the moment had passed. Jess had wiped it away as easily as she'd wiped away her tears, no more talk of mums or what that might mean. He didn't want to push it any further. Complicated didn't come close. But the thought of Jess being a mum to Lucy still lingered in his head.

He looked at her beautiful shining eyes and knew she was making the best of things. Had put on her happy face. Who was he to take that away? He grinned back. 'She did not fancy me. She just meant well.'

'She meant a lot of things.' Jess nudged him. 'One of which was *What are you doing later*?'

Trying to quell his smirk, he winked. 'Now who's being Dr Territorial?'

The excitement caught up with the toddler in the tiny planetarium cinema as an alien took them on a tour to outer space. Wedged between her father and Jessie, Lucy slipped into a peaceful sleep on the reclining seats.

The blacked-out room was almost empty and the show, more suitable for kids than adults, didn't capture Jessie's interest. Instead, she found herself fixated on Luke's profile, his strong nose, carved chin. His mouth twitched into a smile and he turned, caught her looking at him.

Her stomach somersaulted at his easy smile, the softness in his eyes. But the longer he held her gaze, the more the swirly feeling shifted to something deeper. Not just desire but visceral need.

When had that happened? This need? She couldn't pinpoint one specific moment, it had crept on her more stealthily than that. The kindness he extended her. His laughter at her lame jokes. So much so she wanted to make him laugh even more, just to watch the tilt of that adorable mouth and the spark in his eyes.

Which made the thought of it ending slice her like a knife. But she had to go. She couldn't stay. Couldn't give him what he deserved.

Lucy's innocent question earlier had sent shockwaves spiralling through her. If only you could just choose yourself a mother. Choose yourself a life. If only things could be as simple as a three-year-old wanted them to be.

But they weren't.

Life was messy and peppered with regrets and mistakes.But surely savouring Luke couldn't be a mistake. Enjoying some loving wasn't a mistake. If nothing else, these people had taught her so much about caring and growing and reaching out to people. That couldn't be a mistake. It was an experience she would cherish on her travels, not something she would regret. She tried to pull her gaze away from him but, just like leaving, it was so much harder than she thought. A wry smile caught his lips. He whispered, 'What are you looking at?'

'You,' she mouthed back, as if that was the most obvious thing in the world.

Luke stared right on back, trying to fathom her out. What was she thinking? What did she want? Him? To stay? Or, like Chloe, was she only happy with a plane ticket in her pocket?

So many emotions warred inside him. Loyalty to Lucy, that was big. Lust for Jess—sure as all hell. What sane man wouldn't want to make love to her?

The one that won outright was a deep tenderness. Strange. He'd never felt that so keenly before. Not with Chloe, nor any of his other…conquests. This thing with Jess threw him so far offside he could barely think straight.

On impulse he reached his hand across the seat to touch Jess's arm. But quickly pulled it back. No, he couldn't act on impulse. Years ago that was all that had driven him to a trail of one-night stands and short-lived romances.

He looked at the sleeping child between them,

the result of his carelessness. This was his priority. Not some woman who was passing through.

And yet, compared to all those half-hearted flings, compared to Chloe, Jess was worth more than every impulse he'd ever had.

She was one hell of a woman. How could he keep his distance? There'd be distance enough next week when she was in the South Island. Too much distance.

Carefully lifting Lucy into a seat on the other side of him, he edged next to Jessie. 'Hey.'

'Boring film, right?' she said.

'Not as interesting as looking at you.'

'Have I got spinach in my teeth or something?'

'No. And even if you did I wouldn't care. You're pretty perfect any way.'

Her breath hitched as she felt his warm hand curl around hers, every tiny cell responding to his touch. She prised open his fingers and stroked the raised skin where his stitches had been.

The bandage that had kept his dressing in place had long gone, but the puckered scar tissue was still evident as she ran her fingertips from his thumb to his little finger.

How far they'd come since his injury, how tempted and how restrained. How very grown-up and responsible. She'd never fought so much to keep a lid on her feelings, and had never wanted a man more.

His breath stuttered as she pressed her lips against the base of his thumb and traced her tongue along the suture line. Then she held his hand against her mouth and closed her eyes, wishing. Just wishing this could last for ever. All too soon he tugged his hand away, and she turned to him, half-shadowed, silhouetted by a million magic twinkling stars, as a dog alien character recited the names of the planets. She felt empty inside and craved his touch. He held her gaze. A tacit awareness pooled inside her. Urgent. Impatient. Hot. Her pulse quickened. Cheeks blazed.

It was mirrored in his eyes. It was ridiculous to want this. Madness, and yet there was no way she could stop it.

'Jess. That was so unfair,' Luke breathed against her ear as they returned to the foyer, bright sunshine and fresh air. 'Now I want to kiss you all over again.'

'That was the idea,' she whispered back, sneaking her hand into his and wondering where her sense of propriety and sanity had gone. This guy made her think crazy things. Do crazy things, believe in another universe where all things could be possible.

'Later?'

Drawing in a ragged breath, she felt the surge of desire almost overwhelm her. She couldn't fight this need for him any longer, couldn't assuage this thirst for his touch. They'd crossed a line. She knew she was plunging them into dangerous terrain. Knew that one look at her scars would have him running, and that once he knew her secret he'd be glad to see her go. But there was no way she could stop this wild trajectory. Just for one night she would have him.

She answered him with words as blatant as the fire his eyes. 'Yes, Luke. Later.'

'Dinner?' Luke asked at the threshold of his house, opening the door and letting his daughter race upstairs.

A seemingly innocent question but it offered so much more than food. Jessie saw the flash of awareness in his eyes. There was definitely nothing innocent about it.

'Are you sure?' She tried for nonchalant, but her words came out wobbly, just like her smile.

'Never been more sure. You?'

A weird buzz of excitement frothed through her. If she walked through this door there would be no going back. She'd already got so close to the edge she may just as well jump right over. Scars and all. To hell with it. She'd be gone by next weekend. Would never have to face him again. 'Yes, dinner would be lovely.'

'It won't be a big deal, but if you give me a few minutes I'll throw something together.'

'A man who can throw something together should never be turned down. I can't remember the last time anyone cooked for me.' Let alone a guy. 'You really are a man of talents.'

'You'd better believe it.' He gave her a slow wink and his gaze dipped to her T-shirt. A slow heat suffused her skin. Just the thought of his hand near her breast earlier made her shudder with anticipation.

He tipped his head and kissed her on her mouth. She opened her lips and relished the touch of his tongue flicking against hers. Hot and hungry.

'We could just skip to dessert,' he groaned into her mouth.

'Hmm. Things are always better on a full stomach.' She pushed him into the hall, loving his wicked edge. Something she'd never imagined possible a fortnight ago. 'Get a wriggle on, I'm starving.'

'Daddy, help me do paintin',' Lucy called from her room.

Jessie sighed and followed him into the house. 'Where does she get her energy from?'

'Beats me. But she's all front and no substance. She'll be comatose by eight.'

Jessie looked at her watch. Just an hour away. Could she manage an hour without touching him again?

'I'll come up in a second, sweetheart, I'm just sorting dinner.' Rubbing his hand over his chin, he gave Jessie a half-smile. 'Sorry about this. Torn between entertaining a three-year-old angel and a twenty-eight-year-old temptress. Who'd believe it? I promised I'd do some painting with her. She got a new easel for her birthday.'

'You cook. I'll paint.' She turned to him as she hit the second stair. 'And don't ever apologise for her.' He'd thought Lucy would be the reason Jess wouldn't want to hang around. Had heard how hard it was for solo dads, had even experienced the brush-off from single women uninterested in kids.

But if anything, between him, Jess and Luce it was becoming two against one. And he was the one!

He watched her sashay up the stairs. The swing of her backside tugged at his groin. He wanted her so much it hurt, wanted to bury himself deep inside her—that was a given. But there was more

here. Jess was special. He had tried to guard his
heart, but hadn't expected to like her so much.

A few seconds later an excited, paint-splattered
Lucy grabbed Jessie's hand and dragged her out
onto the little verandah that jutted off her hot pink
bedroom. 'I done this for you, Jess.'

'Why, thank you.' Jessie stared at the splodges
and swirls on the paper, ruing her decision to come
upstairs.

Maybe she'd have been better with the cooking. She needed someone to help with translation.
Toddler art was a foreign language, and as far as
she was concerned this painting looked like a couple of sperm caught in a tornado.

'It's a lovely picture, Lucy. Tell me all about it.'
She'd heard that technique from one of the practice nurses and it seemed to work well.

Lucy grinned and pointed to a small splotch.
'That's me.'

'Of course. I can see the pink dress.' Jessie stared
even harder, but the rest may as well have been
Swahili.

'Daddy.' A large grey blob.

'I can see how much bigger he is than you. Of
course.'

'And dat's you, holding my hand.'

'Me? Oh, yes. The green one. How clever.'

'And dat's…' The little girl's toothy grin broadened as she squealed with delight at a silvery squiggle. 'The Man in the Moon.'

Jessie's heart tightened as she pulled the little girl into her arms and squeezed her close, relishing the little wriggle, the soft sun-lotion smell of her, the freshness of her skin. 'You gorgeous girl.'

She sighed and let her go. Swallowing back the tinge of sadness at the thought of leaving, Jessie rubbed her hands together. She took a paintbrush and painted the whole of her left hand in silvery grey. 'Let's do some palm prints.'

'Oh, okay.' Lucy's mess of curls bobbed up and down as she copied Jessie and pressed her painted hand onto a clean sheet of paper. 'That right, Jess?'

'Great stuff. Let's do another one. Look, my hand is so much bigger than yours.' Jess pressed her hand hard on the paper, again and again. Lucy laughed along with her, making her own prints with delighted enthusiasm.

A clash of cooking pots downstairs had the little girl dashing from the deck into her bedroom. Her chubby legs and serious frown melted Jessie's heart just a little bit more. She was so cute.

'Daddy! Daddy… Oh. Ohh.'

A pause.

Then a whimper.

Jessie ran into the bedroom and found the little tyke curled up on the floor by the door. Her bottom lip protruded and she looked as if her world had come tumbling down. 'Hey, what's the matter, Luce? You hurt yourself?'

'I did an oh-oh.'

'A what?'

Lucy pointed to the wall. A perfect silver handprint adorned the too-bright sickly pink wallpaper.

Jess couldn't help but smile. It might be the end of a three-year-old's world, but it was an easy mess to remedy. 'Oh, gosh. So you did.'

'Daddy be cross.'

'No, he won't. How could he ever be cross with you?' Jessie laughed as she looked longer at the shocking pink wall and the shimmery contrast of the silver. It looked kind of nice. Amateur, but nice. A tiny flicker of light inside her grew into a shining idea. 'Actually, this is perfect.'

This would be something for Luke to remember her by.

His footsteps echoed on the wooden floorboards as he wandered through the house, clattering plates. Any minute now he would call them down for dinner. Delicious garlic and cumin smells wafted through the house, reminding her of the back streets of Jaipur. The usual call of wander-lust seemed dimmed today; the lure of exotic India didn't feel so acute.

She wondered if there was a connection between those two trains of thought.

'We don't have much time.' Jessie pressed her damp palm onto the wall next to Lucy's print. It wasn't as bright as Lucy's. She needed more paint. 'Quick! Watch this.'

She darted across the room, grabbed the paint pot and painted another palm print. Lucy's eyes widened in utter shock and horror, and glee.

By the time Luke had made it to the bedroom a quarter of the wall was covered in silvery prints. 'Hey, you two. Thought we'd have a picn—' A deep line appeared over his forehead and his face reddened. 'What is this?'

Jessie swallowed and shuffled Lucy behind her. Maybe this wasn't such a great idea after all. 'I just thought…well, oh, what the heck. Luke, this room needed sorting out. Way too much pink. And we did it. I did it.'

She folded her arms across her chest and flashed him a don't-you-dare-upset-Lucy glare.

He paced around the room, loosening his shoulders, obviously trying to quell whatever irritation rippled through him. He stopped in front of the wall and stared some more. His throat bobbed up and down as the silver handprints glinted in the dappled sunlight, mocking him.

'Well, you did agree the pink could do with toning down a bit.' Jessie held her breath.

'You could have asked first.'

'Come on, Luke. It's just paint. We were having fun.'

Jessie crossed her fingers and showed them to Lucy. The little girl did the same. They stood and held their breath and waited.

Then Luke took a hold of Lucy's wrist, scrutinised her palm. He measured it against his.

He did the same to Jessie's.

As she felt his smooth skin touch hers she willed him to be happy. Or at least pretend to be happy. 'I'm sorry,' she whispered. 'I thought I was doing the right thing.'

For a few seconds he just looked at her with a bemused frown. Then, silently and very slowly, he painted his palm with silver. And, oh, so deliberately pressed his hand above one of Lucy's prints.

A small bubbling giggle erupted from Lucy's lips. 'Oh-oh. Daddy did it too.'

Taking his hand from the wall, his face lightened into a huge grin and a guffaw sprang from deep within his chest. 'He certainly did, darling.

And doesn't it look great? Come on, let's do some more.'

Jessie hesitated. She'd meant to do a small corner that could easily be painted over. 'Perhaps we shouldn't get carried away. Are you sure?'

'Aw, Jess. Don't be a spoilsport.' He hoisted Lucy up so she could reach a higher spot. A genuine mischievous glow sparked in his eyes. 'This is great, isn't it, squirt?'

'Funny Daddy.' Lucy giggled as she pressed her hand against the wall.

As he turned and winked at her Jessie's heart filled with hope. This was the first time she'd seen him so relaxed and easy with his daughter. Seemed he'd finally grasped the concept of fun. And there wasn't a parenting book in sight.

Within minutes the wall was redecorated in small, medium and large prints.

Luke stood back and admired their work then he swooped Lucy into one arm, curled his other round Jessie. Wrapped them to his chest and held them tight. 'I don't know. You guys will be the death of me.'

When Luke's chin rested on the crown of her head, so casually and effortlessly, when Lucy's tiny hand curled into hers, so trusting and accepting, Jessie's stomach constricted.

This glimpse of family life was a gift, a blessing. Silly, fun, courageous. Forgiving and tender. A fleeting moment she'd treasure for ever. This was what she'd be walking away from.

It was getting harder by the second.

'I was shocked at first. But I listened to you.' Luke confessed to Jess later as they sat in his garden on a blanket in the shade of an ancient pohutukawa tree. Its crimson flowers lay around their feet like confetti. He grimaced at the analogy. As if. Jess would have roses with added thorns for her wedding bouquet, just to prick him with. For fun.

Why the hell did weddings suddenly spring to mind? Considering he'd sworn off marriage after Chloe, it seemed strange his thoughts swung that way today. Or did it? With Jess in his garden, sitting under his tree, drinking his wine, her silhouette framed in the dying rays of the sun. Right now anything could be possible.

She looked as stunning as ever in an old T shirt and fatigues, now splattered with silver paint. Her hair hung down her back, loose and carefree, but she seemed distracted.

He tried to pull her back from whatever daydream she was walking in. 'Jess? I must admit the room really does look better. Not so…'

'Pink?' She finally gave him her attention and gifted him a smile.

He took it gladly and let its warmth suffuse his skin.

'Yes. And Lucy loves it. I think she knew we'd done something wicked and fun and was just as entranced as me. So long as she doesn't think she's got carte blanche to redecorate every time she gets her paints out.'

He remembered his little girl's shining face as she, for once, went to bed on time, did as she was asked and even took her spacer without arguing. Jess may not think she was Mary Poppins, but she'd worked magic around his little girl.

And around him too. No one else had opened him up to so much fun. She was right, he needed to live a little more and worry a little less. Although that was hard to master.

'So, Jess. Tell me about Vietnam. Why there?'

She took a sip of wine and sifted a handful of pohutukawa threads through her fingers, let them fall to the earth. 'I kind of fell into it really, but soon got hooked. I was travelling around Asia and thought maybe I could do some good while I was there.'

'And what did you do exactly?'

'I started working for a local homeless charity.

The fallout from the war is still immense even after all this time. People were displaced, injured and there's no consistent care available.' The sun had dipped behind the house, leaving a cool breeze around their shoulders. Jessie shivered.

It seemed natural to pull her close. She nuzzled against him, fitting perfectly between his out-stretched legs. He leaned back against the tree. She lay on him, her weight just right. 'Then I got sucked into visiting orphanages, doing outreach work. That was heartbreaking but somehow ad-dictive.'

'I can imagine.'

'There are so many homeless kids there. Half of them have parents, but they just can't afford to keep them.'

She sighed at the memory and stifled the ache in her heart for those kids. It had been so diffi-cult at first, seeing all those children abandoned by their parents. Fresh from her accident, she had hardly been able to bear to see babies so malnour-ished and dirty and she'd wanted to bring them all home. Elderly care and rehab had been so much easier to deal with.

'The ones with parents have their heads shaved but they leave three tufts of hair so they can be identified as unavailable for adoption. The ones available for adoption have their heads shaved completely.'

'Sounds hard.'

'It was, but immensely rewarding.'

'You need to get back there?'

'I'd love to, once I've got the money together. I'd love to go back to India too. But there are plenty of other places needing decent medical care.'

She snuggled against the thick heat of him. Strange to be talking about leaving yet sharing this connection.

The sunset had dissolved into a rage of black clouds. A metallic tang filled the air, mingling with the garlic and exotic spices. The breeze dropped, leaving a strange, heavy calm hanging around them like a shawl.

'North Beach must seem tame in comparison. You'll be glad to go?'

'No. North Beach has been wonderful. I'll miss it.' *I'll miss you.* She craned her neck to look at him and tried to tell him what she meant. How she felt. But she didn't even know herself. Apart from confused and excited and comfortable and dangerous. Was there one word to sum that up? Hell if she knew.

'You do a damn fine feast, Dr McKenzie.' She

slithered forward, stuck a chunk of ciabatta into the dip and wrapped her teeth around it.

Mesmerised by the action, Luke couldn't help staring.

She licked her lips. 'Yum. I can't believe the flavours, salty and lemony, and the garlic is divine. Who'd have ever thought of making hummus hot? Very clever.'

'It's only from a recipe. No big deal.' Although the swell of pride at her words was like a power punch.

'And these prawns are gorgeous.' She tore off a pink head and sucked at the body then licked her fingers one by one.

'Here, let me do that.' He couldn't resist. Saw the flash of heat in her eyes.

He took hold of her middle finger and slowly sucked the tip.

'Luke!' The word came out on a gasp but she very definitely didn't remove her finger from his mouth. She kept her gaze on him, watching intently as he dipped his tongue around the phalanx of the finger. Her pupils flared. Her lips parted.

One, two, three thick drops of rain hammered onto the blanket, making them jerk up, laugh and stare skywards. Jessie started to gather the remains of the food. 'Quick. It's going to pour. Let's get inside.'

Within minutes they were splashing through rivulets of water in a tropical downpour, arms filled with plates and bottles, the blanket dragged through a puddle. Jessie's eyes gleamed with delight. Her head tipped back and she laughed, a delightful sound, like music.

'Just like the monsoon.' She did a dainty pirouette, balancing the plates in a wobbly stack. 'But in Vietnam we don't run, we dance.'

At the laundry door Luke stopped. He put his bundle on the floor then took the things Jessie was carrying out of her hands. Fire burnt inside him as he watched her.

The rain beat down, slicking her T-shirt to her breasts, her combats moulded to the shape of her legs. Her hair hung like rat's tails, wild and out of control. Water dripped from her nose, her eyelashes. She did a jerky dance, arms outstretched, head tipped back. She had never looked more beautiful.

'To what tune?' He took her hands and waltzed her round and round.

'Ah, I don't know—anything. There was a man lived in the moon? Joke.'

'And now it'll be stuck in my head all night.

Thanks.' He wound her round more slowly, watching sheer happiness caught in her face. She threw her head back and caught raindrops in her mouth as if they were the last drink on earth. It was the first time he'd ever seen her so utterly unguarded and relaxed.

Then she wrapped her arms round his neck, pressed her nose against his, stared up at him with I-want-you eyes, and the world stopped.

But they just went on spinning. Just the two of them. In this time and this magical moment. Nothing else existed except this slice of joy in his garden. This was how he would remember her when she was gone. Drenched and laughing and carefree and gazing at him with those eyes that spoke to his deepest need.

She ground to a halt, suddenly serious. 'Stop, stop, I'm getting dizzy.'

'And you're making me dizzy.' Cupping her face in his hands, he pressed his lips against hers and kissed her with every piece of his heart.

'Here, let's get you out of those wet things.'

'Mmm. Let's.' Somehow Jessie found herself in Luke's bedroom. The kissing had continued as they'd fumbled their way upstairs, trying not to wake Lucy.

Very gently he lifted Jessie's arms, his fingers grazing her skin as he peeled the T-shirt from her goose-bumps and over her head.

'Now these.' He reached to unzip her trousers.

For a second her mind registered his movements, but the happy haze—maybe the wine too—blurred them. He was undressing her?

Good.

Good?

Her mind sharpened. Her scars. If she could get through this without him seeing them, then she would treasure this night for ever. If not, then she'd let fate guide her. Either way, she was lost and couldn't stop what was inevitable. She had to have him.

But she had to give herself a fighting chance. Undress herself. In the dark. She grabbed her zip and pushed his hand away. 'No.'

'It's okay, darling Jess. Please hurry, before you catch hypothermia.'

'Please, Luke. No.'

'Have it your own way, then.' He laughed, caught her legs in the crook of his elbow and swung her into his arms.

When he reached the shower he placed her gently on the floor and switched on the faucet. 'You need to get warm.' Hot water cascaded between them. Steam swirled around as he gazed at her. Not touching, but she ached for his fingers. Not speaking, but she longed to hear his voice. Hardly daring to breathe. Each inhalation ragged and quickening.

And he just went right on looking at her as if she was a goddess.

When she'd stopped shaking he leaned away from her, found some shampoo and massaged it into her hair.

The pressure from his fingers on her scalp sent shivers of desire reaching further and further down her spine, pooling in the small of her back.

She relished this moment of utter bliss. Being with him was reckless. But with his hands tangled in her hair and the heat of him warming her cold bones, it felt so right.

'You okay?' he whispered, as he rinsed off the bubbles and smoothed his fingertips through the ends of her hair.

'Uh-huh,' she murmured, barely able to speak with the lightness from his touch. 'Just dandy.'

Palming her cheek, he gazed at her. 'Did I tell you how much I want you?'

'Not out loud.' She stared back up at him. At his lovely steady gaze from intense blue-grey eyes and the golden sparks that told her how much he cared.

And feeling his hardness between them, she knew how much he wanted her. 'But I get the message.'

Her arousal arrowed out to her legs, her nipples, her mouth.

She pressed closer, moving her hips against his tight, wet jeans, as the long-held promises and trying so hard to keep away from him melted into nothing.

His face moved closer, his lips a heartbeat away. His breath caressed her neck, making her curl instinctively to him.

'God, I want you so much,' he groaned, then he claimed her mouth, hard and greedy.

She opened her mouth to his and he licked his tongue against hers, sending quivers of delight through her nipples and her abdomen.

They fell against the glass as Jessie ran her hand down his stomach and pulled at the fabric of his shirt, tried to tug it up his body. But cracked her elbow hard against the shower screen. 'Ouch.'

Luke planted a kiss on her elbow and laughed. 'This isn't going to work. Let's get out of here.'

'Race you.' She pushed open the door, still entwined in his arms.

'Don't dare go anywhere without me.'

'Where would I go without you?' she breathed, and held out her hand to him.

Half in and half out of the cubicle, he grasped her arms, raised them above her head and leaned her against the wall, holding her captive as he kissed a trail down her neck to her bra. His teeth gently bit through the fabric, grazed the hard bud, firing shockwaves through her. The world reeled sideways as she pressed harder against him. When he'd kissed a divine track over the other nipple he tipped his damp head to her. 'Okay. Bed. Now.'

Somehow they staggered to the bed, laughing and wet and hot and tangled. His hands cupped her buttocks as he laid her on the crisp white sheets, looking, just looking at her with such heat in his eyes.

And whatever he couldn't say with words he told her in that look. This moment. *This*. This was for them. Forget what the future held. Forget the past. *This*. This was theirs. A deep, almost animal moan came from somewhere and she realised it was her. All rational thought, all words had fled her. He kissed her again, hard and long, bruising her lips. He tugged at the zipper on her trousers.

Oh, God.

She drew away from him. 'Switch the lamp off. Please. Don't look.'

His hand stilled but his breathing quickened. 'What is it, Jess?'

Embarrassment ripped through her. Most women had big bottoms or fat thighs they didn't want on show. Nothing as disfigured as this. It reminded her of so much sorrow, a time when her heart had been broken so badly she didn't think she'd ever mend.

'The car accident? It was a bit more than I let on.'

He pulled away a little and she wondered whether she should have told him. Maybe he would never have noticed. Yeah, right.

'Are you okay, though?' Stroking her ribcage with his fingers and his soft gentle voice soothing her, she was filled with a yearning to tell him everything. To lay herself bare, literally.

'Does it hurt?'

'What a way to kill a moment.' She forced out a laugh. If she didn't tell him soon she felt like she might explode. 'A piece of metal from the van I hit pierced my belly. There are scars.'

'That explains it.' He stroked along her arm, the pain in his eyes genuine. No pity. Just pain, for her.

'What?'

'The way you touch your stomach when you're nervous. You still feel it.'

She ran her hand to her stomach and smiled. 'You're right, I do. Transparent, eh? They're not pretty.'

'And you thought, what? That it might put me off?' He wriggled closer, faced her, took her hand in his and kissed it. 'It'd take more than a few old scars to put me off.'

'But…still…you never know.'

'Is that why you keep holding out on me? Why didn't you tell me before?'

'Because…' Michael hadn't been able to look at her after the accident, after everything. Couldn't take the woman she'd become. And he'd found solace in the admin assistant and absolution in their divorce. 'Not everyone is as understanding as you.'

'Jess, I'd never hurt you, you've got to believe that.' He switched the lamp off, the room lit now only by moonlight. He touched a finger to her swollen lips, traced it slowly down her chin. Then paused, keeping his eyes fixed on hers. She watched him with a mix of horror and desire in her gaze.

Now Luke knew why she'd been so scared of anything intimate. He'd hurt her, the ex. Left her embarrassed and ashamed. Anger swelled like a tidal wave through him. 'Trust me, Jess. Let it go.'

This mattered. He needed to make her believe him. 'You are truly beautiful, inside and out. You bring such joy to people's lives. Mine. Lucy's.' He tapped her gently on the chin. 'I'm crazy about you.

More than crazy.' He could feel her body tremble as very slowly he tipped his lips to the soft skin in the dip between her divine breasts.

'Luke, you—'

'Hush.' He licked a nipple, enjoying the quick hardening. Enjoying the pleasure he gave her that made her arch closer, loved the fire in her eyes. He wanted to take it slowly, wishing this moment could last for ever, yet his body strained for her touch, his senses sizzling and burning, and he ached to be inside her.

'This isn't about me, it's for you. I'm crazy about you because you are a beautiful woman.'

The muscles in her stomach involuntarily clenched as his trail took him down to the top of her pants. He ran his tongue back along the dip under her ribs. She tried to sit up, ran her fingers over his chest. A small amount of pressure on her sternum convinced her to lie back. 'Stay still.'

Carefully, so as not to stress her more, he edged the trousers and her knickers over her hips and onto the floor. The dark lines of her scars ridged her pale skin. 'Jess. Nothing about you is ugly. You are crazy and wild and wonderful.'

He nuzzled his erection against her naked thigh, making her gasp.

'And one hell of a sexy woman.'

'But—'

'But nothing.' He nudged against her again. 'Does my body say I want you?'

'I…I don't know.'

'Jess? Give me a break here. You've done gynae. You know how this whole thing works. I want you. My body wants you. Feel it.' He pressed against her one more time. 'Say it.'

'You…?'

'Say it.'

She sighed and her breathing stalled. 'You want me.'

'Hell, yes.'

Running his tongue in tentative circles against the gnarled skin, he kissed her devastated body. In the darkness he couldn't make out the extent of the damage, but felt the edge of where the peachy skin melted into a criss-cross of lines.

'This is you, Jess. You are strong and brave. These scars are part of you, but they're not all of you. You are perfect and I want you. More than anything in the world.'

The muscles in her arm tensed as she tried to push him away. 'But I don't know how you can find me attractive. It's like a road map of spaghetti junction.'

'Then it's bringing me home.'

He kissed her again, slowly and gently. A deep caress that offered her his promise. He would never hurt her. Gradually he heard the sigh, felt her relax and buck against him. Finally, she believed him.

She deepened the kiss, hot and hungry now, a soft moan escaping her lips. 'I want you, Luke.'

Her breasts swelled against him, her hand trembled as she undid the zipper on his jeans. Then she took his erection in her hand. He groaned in delight. 'That's my girl.'

'And I need you inside me.'

'Are you sure?' But he was already way too gone with need for her. Her lovely mouth reached for his, her hands gripped his hips to hers so he could feel the warmth and the wetness, and he was almost undone.

'Now, Luke. I need you now.' She giggled and stroked his tongue with hers. 'I double dare you.'

'That's so not fair. Slow down, darling Jess.'

'We can do slow next time,' she sighed into his ear, then licked his neck, and he could taste her and feel her and smell that flowery scent.

Hell, yes. 'And the time after that...'

She was in his arms and in his bed. She was so alive and vibrant and just...Jess. So small beneath him, but so much of everything he'd always wanted. 'I'll just grab my condoms.'

'No need. It's safe.'

He pulled back. No way would he take any risks with her. Or with himself. One unplanned pregnancy was enough. 'You sure?'

'Now you have to trust me,' she said, and shifted, and then he was almost there, nudging inside her, as if in a dream. Only this was better than a dream, because it was real. And she was already promising they could do it again. 'It's safe.'

He thrust slowly into her, stroking her hair away from her eyes. 'Jess. Jess.'

Her beautiful sensual eyes, which reached to the depths of his soul, told him in so many ways how she felt about him.

She gripped his face and kissed him again, long and hard, rising with him in perfect time, staring up at him with a passion and a love that could no longer be denied.

Because there was no other word to describe it. It was in her face, and it was there, like a tiny jewel, glittering in his heart.

With relief and joy and shock he finally made sense of everything. He loved her.

It was a few minutes before he could think or speak. 'You okay, Jess?'

A knot tightened in his chest. He couldn't love

her. A fun romance, sure. Intense, vibrant, absolutely.

But love? That was not supposed to happen. That was a place he didn't want to go.

He didn't know what to do next. All out of bright ideas. Loving someone who was leaving in, what? Six days? *Great one, Einstein.*

Did he want to talk? No.

Did he want to sleep? No.

Did he want to love her? Yes. No. Yes. *Damn.* Of course he did.

But he couldn't ask her to give up her amazing life for him here in sleepy North Beach. That had backfired spectacularly once. *I'm not the settling-down type, Luke.* He wasn't going there again.

'Ah, yes.' She wriggled closer, fitting perfectly into the crook of his arm, her blonde curls tickling his cheek. He could feel her tight yawn, then the curve of her smile against his heart.

She whispered, 'That was yummy.'

'You want to talk some more?'

'Why? Do you want to roll over and go to sleep?' Her hair bled onto his pillow like a blonde stain, her limbs tangled in his sheets. Her smell bruised his skin. It should be perfect.

Only it wasn't.

She snagged his arm with her hand and giggled.

'Isn't that what you're supposed to do? Roll over? Or smoke a cigarette? Men are from Venus, right?'

'I think it's Mars. I thought you were the astronomy geek.'

'I'm not sure there was a lot of astronomy involved. Lots of star gazing perhaps.' She kissed along his chest, tweaked one of his nipples with her teeth. Shafts of desire arced along his groin. He inched away. She didn't seem to notice. 'I enjoyed today, Luke.'

'Me too.'

God, he had no idea what the hell to do now. Way out of his depth, and then some. He shifted, hitched up onto his elbow and ran his free hand over the roughened skin of her belly. Her battle scars.

He was lost, startled by his urgent need for her. Humbled by her scarring. Paralysed at the thought of her gone, and what that would do to his daughter, and himself. 'That woman was right, Lucy does kind of smile like you. You're great with her. You ever thought about settling down? Having a family?'

Her shoulders stiffened, her jaw muscles clenched. The tension was palpable. She edged away, sat up in bed and pulled the sheets over her. The space where she'd been was suddenly cold. He wished he could take it back. Rewind to the heat of their lovemaking.

'No. That's impossible.'

'Oh. Okay.' He'd blown it. *Don't clip my wings, I need to fly.* Chloe's last words to him echoed in his head. 'I guess your job's pretty full on.'

'Luke.' She hunched away from him, knowing the pain would be deep in her eyes. Knowing that this could have been her chance for a future with him. Shocked at how much it hurt when she'd believed she'd dealt with it. Shocked that now it mattered. Now all the pain she'd hidden for so long brimmed to the surface.

'That accident? I was pregnant, with a little girl. She didn't make it.'

'God, Jessie, I'm so sorry.'

She could feel his pity now, coating his sigh. Couldn't quite read the look on his face in the half-light. She closed her eyes. It was easier to talk that way. Easier to block out the tears. 'Yes, me too.'

'How far along were you?'

'Twenty-two weeks.'

He reached a warm hand to her thigh and stroked. 'That must have been hell.'

'Yeah.'

His physical connection was surprisingly tender. So long she'd survived this on her own. To share it with someone else was a relief. She swallowed back the lump lodged hard in her throat. Being pregnant had been her only experience of having an anchor. The only thing that had ever tempted her to stop travelling. She'd tried to make a home with Michael. But that had disintegrated the second she'd lost her child. He'd fled into the arms of another woman, unable to even look at his wife. She'd had an accident, lost their baby and lost her future all at once.

'Took a bit of therapy. And a lot of time out. But it's okay now. I have my scan pictures…' She had other photos too, taken as her daughter had died, but couldn't bring herself to look at them now. Remembering her baby vital, kicking and tumbling, caused less pain.

'And just knowing she was here…' Running a hand over her belly, she smiled. 'That helps. It's just such a shame.'

'I can't imagine what it was like. The second I knew I had a child my heart just melted. To have lost her would have been unbearable.'

Her lip trembled but she'd promised not to cry any more.

'It's odd, the things you remember through that weird haze of desperate grief. No one warned me how much I'd dream about her. Or told me what to do with the tiny doll-like clothes we didn't need any more. How she had eyelids and fingernails, even though she was so little. How perfect she was.' How Jessie's splintered heart would never truly heal.

Luke reached out and pulled her back to him and she let him spoon his body around hers. His lips brushed her neck, his heart beat against her back. Strong. Steady. Constant.

'Did you name her?'

The pain was unbearable. A full ache that washed over her body and settled back in her bones. The longing to hold her daughter had been almost over-whelming. How empty her arms and her body had felt. But that had been nothing compared to her heart.

She tried to weigh the word around in her mouth after so long. To say the name that had held so much promise and such sorrow. 'Charlotte.'

'Pretty.'

'She was. Tiny and perfect.' And she'd never told anyone that before. 'Only Michael knew her name.' And when he'd left she'd had no one to talk to about it, no one to share the memories of her daughter.

'You've been so brave, Jessie. Carrying that around with you for so long.'

His voice was so velvet soft, like a feathery kiss, that she was lulled into telling him the rest. She took a steadying breath, feeling her ribcage swell against his chest, safe in his arms. She chewed her lip. May as well tell the whole truth now. There was nothing left to hide. An open book, albeit battered and torn.

'I can't have any more babies, Luke. The piece of metal pierced my uterus. The docs thought they might be able to repair it for a future pregnancy, but an infection spread, and in the end they had to take everything away. So no. I can't think about settling down. Or families. Because it's not something I can have.'

The night beat around them, in the leftover warmth of their lovemaking and the fading thrum of their urgent desire. In the imprint of his hand on her thigh, the pink flush of their skin. In the unanswered question of *where to next*?

He said nothing. What was there to say? What could he do? Except hold her tight in the dark and never let go.

CHAPTER ELEVEN

BY THE time Jess woke Luke had gone. She missed him already. The sheets were rumpled but empty, with just a trace of his scent. Listening hard for his footsteps, she made sure he wouldn't catch her doing something…silly as she picked up his pillow and inhaled deeply. Committing the smell to memory. Cinnamon, spice, *us*.

A glance at the clock told her she'd slept late.

She'd also slept well. At least, eventually, after he'd woken her in the night to make good on her promise of slow and sexy.

An aroma of toast and fresh coffee filled the air, and her stomach rumbled. She stretched out on Luke's king-size bed and wriggled her toes, eased out the exercise-induced knots.

She tried to fight back the rise of hope that swelled her chest and fitted comfortably on her face in a smile. It had been wonderful. He had been wonderful.

She'd never believed she could find something

so pure, so *right*. She wanted to drown in more kisses, eat breakfast in bed with him, make love with him some more.

But then, as she took it all in, Luke's scent and their wet piles of clothes, memories of last night intertwined with what had gone before, their separate plans for the future, her stomach tightened in a knot of sadness.

He hadn't said a word about her infertility, just held her in a smog of sexual heat. But what could he have said? That it didn't matter?

Of course it mattered. He had plans for siblings for Lucy, a future filled with kids. She couldn't ask him to give that up.

Besides, the more time she spent with Lucy, the more Jessie's heart ached for the children in those far-away orphanages. Lucy was lucky she at least had one parent to care for her.

A deep, almost tangible sorrow wormed its way into her heart and squashed her smile.

This was such a mistake.

Gorgeous and perfectly heavenly though it was, it was a mistake of epic proportions. She was leaving soon and had determined to do it with everyone's hearts intact.

Her throat clogged with all she going to lose.

This wonderful man, his beautiful daughter. But it had to be done. Didn't it?

Could she stay here? Did he even want her to stay? He'd never mentioned it. If he did, could she allow herself to be lured into a belief that his future didn't matter? That everything she'd worked towards didn't matter?

Hell, no. Through her muddled thoughts she could make out what she needed to do. What she had to do. The right thing.

Taking advantage of the quiet, she tried to work out how to start a conversation that ended in goodbye.

A sudden clatter of teeny footsteps signalled that the end of the quiet would happen any minute…

Now. 'Daddy?'

The tiny tot slammed through the bedroom door dressed in a pair of teddy bear PJs with a white tutu over the top. An incongruous mix. Just like the girl wearing it.

'Oh.' Her nose wrinkled and her angel face broke into a cute smile. 'Jess? Jess! You havin' a snuggle?'

Jess hurriedly pulled the sheet up to her chin and glanced nervously over to her bedraggled clothes strewn over the carpet. Yes, an epic mistake.

'Hey, there. Yes. I just had a quick snuggle, but now it's time to get dressed.'

The little girl didn't seem remotely concerned or confused. She simply climbed up and started to peel back the sheet. 'Can I get in too?'

Whoa. No way, José. 'No sweetheart. I'm just getting up now.'

'Not fair. I want a snuggle.' Undeterred, Lucy gave the sheet a hefty tug, exposing Jess in her full naked glory.

'No!' *My God.* Jess snatched a pillow, covered her boobs with it and dragged the duvet to cover her scars. Where the heck was Luke? She was trapped. She injected a hint of authority into her voice, not to scare or upset Lucy, just to make her stop. 'Sweetie, please. Jess said no.'

'Oh! Jess got a boo-boo?' Lucy pointed to a triangle of bare knobbly scarred flesh. She reached out a finger and prodded it. Then stroked her fingertips over Jess's scarred abdomen. 'You need a kiss better?'

No. No. No. Her heart simultaneously half melting and half freezing at Lucy's tender reaction, Jess wrenched the sheet free and covered herself. Lucy shouldn't be seeing this. She needed jolly, lovely, happy memories, not images of scarred tummies.

She'd faced enough misery to last a lifetime. 'No, thank you. Jess all better now.'

'Poor Jess.' The little tyke's head tilted to one side and her forehead crinkled as she frowned, like she was trying to process what she'd seen. 'Come do some painting?'

What? Jess ran her palm over her forehead and bit back a smile. So much for concern about mentally scarring Lucy for life. How easy to be a toddler where scars and moon men are part of every day's excitement. And just ephemeral interests.

But it was the compassion in the child's face, the relaxed acceptance of the scars and just as easy disinterest in them that pierced Jess's heart. Like her father, Lucy wasn't disgusted or frightened or repulsed. She acknowledged them and moved on.

Jess could learn a lot from that. 'Lovely girl. Lovely Lucy.' She stroked Lucy's cheek, her heart swelling with affection. She swallowed around a lump in her throat. If her baby had survived she'd want her to be just like Lucy. Hell, that feeling in her heart was just as vivid for Lucy as it had been for Charlotte. She'd thought she could never feel like that again. A scary and vulnerable and overwhelming warmth. And an unimaginable ache at the thought of leaving her.

'I have no idea what is going on in that head of

yours. I can't come and paint, love, I need to get dressed.'

Luke arrived in the doorway, carrying a tray of toast and steaming coffee and dressed only in a pair of low-slung board shorts. Fleeting memories of running her tongue along that flat stomach in the middle of the night heated her cheeks.

'Good sleep?' His voice made her heart skip a couple of beats. He handed her a cup of coffee, ruffled his daughter's hair. And smiled.

Was it a good smile? An *it's okay* smile? Giving-anything-away-at-all smile? No. She couldn't read him today. Of all days, today she needed to know what he was thinking.

'I'm sorry, I should have left earlier. It must be a bit weird for Lucy.'

'Don't worry. I'm sure she'll get over it.'

'You think?'

He sat down on the bed and pushed a strand of wayward hair back off her face. Lucy climbed right on up to his lap and grinned at them both.

'I know, kiddo,' he said, as he jiggled his daughter in the air above his head. 'Why don't you go to your room and choose something to wear? Either your rainbow dress or the red spotty one. I'll be along in a minute.'

'And Jess?' The little girl beamed up at them

both, in anticipation, no doubt, of another fun-filled day. 'More painting? Please?'

'No. I think Jess will go home now.' He patted his daughter's bottom and she ran off, singing softly, without a care in the world. Lucky, lucky girl. But, then, she'd already faced enough troubles in her life.

Jess took the hint. Wrapping the sheet tightly around her chest, she went to stand up. 'You're right, I should go.'

'In a minute. I need to talk to you first.'

Ah, so it was a goodbye smile. How could it be anything else? After all, she'd rehearsed her own goodbye lines. She clamped down on the hot sting of tears. She would not cry. Time to drag on the brave face.

He pulled her to sit up in the bed and looked at her with tenderness and desire warring in his eyes. 'About last—'

'God, this sounds like an awful line...don't say it.' She bit against the wobble in her upper lip, forced it to stay taut. Then she pressed a finger to his lips and shivered when he kissed them. The attraction between them was still raw and undeniable. 'It's okay, Luke. I know. It was stupid.'

'It wasn't stupid. Rash, maybe.'

'Regrets?'

He blew on his coffee and shook his head. 'Last night was the best night of my life.'

'But...' Of course there was a *but*. Inevitable. Her heart hammered. It was for the best, she knew it, but that didn't stop it hurting. 'Come on, I'm a big girl now. I shouldn't do things if I can't cope with the fallout.' She squeezed his knee. 'I'm not fragile or broken. I'm over my loss. It's fine.'

He smiled and nodded. 'We need some time. There are things we both have to work through. To be honest, I'm confused. I knew Chloe one whole week before I hung my future on her. I can't do that again. Not for me or for Lucy.'

'And the elephant in the room?'

He frowned. 'What?'

'My infertility. I have nothing more to offer you than what you see, Luke. And you deserve so much more.'

Pushing himself to the bottom of the bed, he sat and faced her, his toes stroking a trail up and down her thigh. The steam from his coffee put him in soft focus. She wanted to always remember him this way. Half-naked, rumpled from lovemaking and tender-hearted.

'Believe me, Jess, you are more than enough.'

'But—'

'But, like I said, there are things we need to think through.'

'Ever sensible.'

'I've got to be. I have Lucy to think about, no matter how much I want you. You have one week left here and, God knows, I want to make the most of every minute. But every minute I spend with you makes me want more.' He stared into the distance. 'You're *leaving*, Jess. So we shouldn't do this again. Not until we know where we're going with it. Not if we both want to get out sane.'

'And, really, we both know there's no future in it,' she said, trying to protect herself. 'It's been fun, though.' Fun? she thought dismally. Sure, she could try to downgrade it to that if it helped her get through. It had been fun, yes, but it had also been incredibly special. Perfect. Just like him.

Everything he'd said was exactly what she'd expected, the same words she'd been just about to use herself. But it didn't stop the shock of tears welling in her eyes or the lump constricting her throat.

He was, oh, so kind. The complete gentleman, the caring lover.

But he didn't ask her stay.

'Luke, sorry to interrupt, but Maggie tells me you're going to see Mr Jenkins.'

'Perfect timing.' He looked up to see Jess peering round the door of his consulting room. Her lips were smudged with her soft rose lipstick, bringing wild memories of their kisses and their one night together. He remembered the taste of that mouth, the silkiness of her hair, and wanted to lose himself in her again. But for their agreement to stay apart...

And the screaming burns patient he was treating. 'I could do with some help.' *Like earplugs.*

'Ouch, poor thing.' Jess pulled a sad face at the harassed-looking mother and her little boy. She looked softly at the ridge of red skin with scattered blisters across the centre of his palm. 'Been in the wars?'

The little guy nodded, stared up at her and stopped crying.

Luke grinned. *Yeah, buddy, she has the same effect on me. Speechless.* 'Barbecue. Superficial dermal burn,' he explained as he swabbed. 'And it's quite sore, isn't it, Callum?'

'Can I put a special dressing on it?' Jess bent over the patient, clearly understanding Luke's shorthand for *not too serious but very painful.* 'Then we can go to the play area until Mum's finished with the boring paperwork stuff. We've got purple lightsabres, you can use your good hand.'

'Purple lightsabres? Cool.'

'So long as you promise to pop back in a couple of days so we can check it again.'

'Will it hurt?'

She fixed her attention solely on the boy, spoke with the soft voice Luke had heard her use with Lucy. The one she hadn't used for the last few days. The one he missed. 'I won't lie to you, it'll hurt a bit. But we need to make it all better. And that means we need to have a quick look. You okay with that, big fella?'

It was her tender, warm voice. Like a mother's voice. A bitter knife twisted in Luke's gut. She'd be a damned fine mother given a chance.

'Okay.' With serious eyes Callum nodded and let her secure a hydrocolloid second skin. 'I s'pose.'

Yep, same effect. Young or old. Has them all eating out of her hand.

After clinic she popped her head round his surgery door again. Dark shadows smudged her eyes, her pout had returned and her mood was obviously as dark as his. Clearly he wasn't the only one not sleeping.

Her cheery mask worked for patients, but he wasn't fooled. She was hurting. Five days ago they'd both said what they thought, and it was pretty much over. Before it had begun, really. Certainly before they'd given it a chance.

Part of him, a lot of him, had hoped she'd come running back into his arms and declare her intention to stay. As if.

He should be relieved he'd had yet another lucky escape from a doomed relationship, so why did fear and love vie inside him? Hell if he knew.

She walked in and closed the door. 'So, Mr Jenkins?'

'Yes, great news. He's been transferred to a medical ward and he's on the mend. Thought I'd go and visit.'

'Why didn't you ask me to come with you?' Tiptoeing her fingers across the desk, she whispered in a gravel voice, 'Are you worried I might seduce you on the way?'

Her sexual gesture was so contrary to her demeanour it was almost ghoulish. Certainly barbed. And fraught with confusion.

Like him. In truth he'd wanted to relish some head space on his own, without being doctor, daddy or downright foolish. Didn't want to have to spend time revisiting a going-nowhere conversation with someone so keen on getting out of his life.

'Of course not.'

'Don't worry, I'll control myself.' She snatched her fingers away. Her mouth was taut and hurt blazed from her eyes. 'I'd like to see him too. It's not often you get the chance to meet a successful cardiac arrest patient.'

The journey was blessedly quick and silent. Once again he had so much to say to her but all the confusion and the love brimmed in his throat, almost choking him.

All the while she just stared ahead, her posture rigid while she fidgeted with her handbag strap. Maybe she, like him, felt tongue-tied and frustrated. Or it could just have been the car phobia thing again.

Hell, he couldn't work her out.

Thankfully, when they arrived at the hospital Mr Jenkins broke the deafening silence with a tired grin and a solid handshake. The fatherly kiss he had for Jess made Luke both proud and sad. He was right, they did make a good team.

'You're looking a bit better than the last time we saw you.' Jess flipped through the old man's charts and gave him a cheeky smile. 'You were a bit…peaky, shall we say?'

'Peaky? You saved my life and I can't thank you both enough. You two, and the surgeons here, whatever they pay you, it should be doubled, trebled.' He rubbed his sternum, which had a thick line of clips running down the middle now, the tell-tale scarring of open heart surgery. 'But, I'm sad to say I think my modelling days are over.'

'Get away with you. Modelling indeed. Couldn't model a lump of clay.' His wife, a quiet, anxious-looking lady who'd so far sat in silence as they'd chatted, put her hand on her husband's.

'He's always been daft. When he came round after the op he told me to phone *Vogue* and cancel the photo shoot. But I keep telling him, scars can be very attractive—shows bravery and strength of character.'

Luke smiled at the old lady. *Couldn't have put it better myself.* Was everything he ever did, every-one he met going to remind him just a little of Jess? 'You'd better watch it, Harold, you'll have to fight the nurses off with a stick with a scar like that.'

Even as he said the words memories of Saturday night tumbled into his head.

Luke caught Jess looking at him. Her eyes smoul-dered, and he had no doubt she too was remember-ing what they'd shared. He hoped that, whatever else happened between them, wherever she went and whatever she did, she at least believed she was beautiful and lovable.

After half an hour of thank-yous and hugs they ambled back to the car.

Jess climbed in. 'Well, that was great. He's a real tonic. And she's a hard case.' She held her palm up. 'High five to us.'

Luke gave her a smile, knowing it was lacklustre, but it was all he could dredge up. He high-fived her. 'Yep. Yay, to us.'

'Wow.' Jess snatched her hand back. The touch of his palm against hers was like an electric force.

'Not just me, then?'

She watched as he started the engine and began to drive. Both hands clutched the steering-wheel, knuckles white, as if holding on was the only way to stay safe. Perhaps he, like her, needed to stay out of touching distance.

'This is too weird.' She'd been avoiding him for days. Had dropped the cosy evenings at his place. Took lonely jogs to work and back and spent the days making small talk in staff meetings, making plans to hand over keys for Zac. But everything she did involved Luke, every action, every memory, every thought. 'Have you had any further thoughts on…you know, us?'

'Non-stop.' He shot her a look that stroked the deepest part of her. 'You?'

'Yeah.' She swallowed deeply. 'Got any answers?'

He shrugged and pulled into the surgery car park. 'Do you mind if I just pop in and grab an inhaler? Lucy's is almost empty and I forgot earlier.'

'No worries. I'll come with you.' Like some kind of celebrity-obsessed teenager she stalked him into the surgery. The thought of not being near him made her feel cold.

Maggie was locking up. 'Just finished the weekly weigh-ins.'

'Sorry?' Jess watched Luke disappear down the corridor and ached to follow him.

'Weight-loss clinic.' The older woman smiled. 'Never mind. Have you forgotten something, dear?'

My mind? 'Just waiting for Luke. He's getting an inhaler. We'll lock up, you go.'

'Don't worry. I know when I'm not needed.' She beamed at Jessie in a sort of satisfied way and left.

'Got it.' He reappeared, brandishing a blue box. His dress shirt pulled taut across the contours of his chest. His stride was languid. He had a way of being efficient yet relaxed. Smiling at her, kind of nonchalant and at ease, he took her breath away. Her legs wobbled. This was what she was leaving behind?

But, then, it wasn't like she had a choice.

'Jess?'

'Let's go.' She grabbed for the doorhandle before she said or did something she'd regret. He covered her hand with his. A sharp jolt of awareness zinged through her veins. And their eyes locked for a crazy second.

If there had been a moment when they could have stopped reaching for each other it didn't register. All she knew, all she felt, all she saw was his mouth only inches away, closing the gap.

'Jess.' His voice was a caress and the only encouragement she needed. 'Just one kiss.'

The kiss was filled with wanting, five days' worth of wishing and a lifetime of need. His hands tangled in her hair, massaged the back of her head, making her feel dizzy and aching for more. She snaked her fingers around his neck, pressing against him. He tasted of nectar and Luke and she ached to quench her thirst.

He ground against her, his hardness between them potent and urgent. Snapping down the blind, he pushed her against the window, his breathing hot and hungry. The aluminium slats clattered noisily under their weight.

'Whoa.' She laughed and raked her nails across his back, pulling at his shirt. His hand trailed slowly down her back, yanked the back of her blouse out of the tuck of her trousers. As his cool palm made contact with her skin, she sucked in a breath.

Dumb and dumber. The thought registered somewhere at the back of her mind, a fragment of doubt that she tried to push away. He was a fine man. Wonderful lover. Heavenly kisser. How could that be dumb?

Would she ever have enough of him? One more kiss. As if. She craved more and more. Would never have enough. Eventually she dragged her mouth away.

They stood, foreheads pressed together while their breathing slowed.

She closed her eyes. Everywhere tingled and ached; this wild need for him singed every part of her.

'We have to stop doing this.' Self-control. That was what he needed. He rubbed his thumb along her swollen lips. Typical he should fall in love with someone who was so damned sensual, and who was moving on shortly. 'We promised.'

'I know.' She bit the corner of her lip and blinked up at him. Her breathing was ragged, his desperation mirrored in her eyes. 'What now?'

'My place?' *Er...self-control?*

Swatting his arm, she laughed. 'You are incorrigible.'

'And you are irresistible.'

She was. A complex whirlwind, all hot and bothered and desperately fighting this as much as he was. He could see indecision in her eyes. He nibbled on her ear and watched the indecision become something much more concrete and enticing.

He thought about the promise in that smile. The hope she offered him with just a glance. His heart kicked.

He was in over his head, the far side of lost. Jess had brought a new direction to his life, fun and joy and an unwavering positivity, despite everything she'd endured.

This wasn't just about making love to her. God, no, it was so much more than that. This was about a future, the two of them. And Lucy.

Together. A family.

How could he let her go?

He'd promised himself he would wait to see how things panned out, weigh up the pros and cons.

But, hell, how to measure the weight of love? Jigsaw pieces slotted together in his brain.

'Jess, I want you so much. Stay?'

His hand slipped to his mouth as he blurted out the unrehearsed words. Damned foolish to risk his heart on her answer. The last time he'd asked that he'd ended up in a failed marriage. Last time had been a duty. But this time…this was a need.

But he'd said it. He couldn't take it back. Wouldn't. He meant it. 'I know it's a big ask. But stay, Jess. Stay here in North Beach.'

'Stay?' Her heart soared. He'd asked her. He wanted her, despite…everything. She stepped away from him. 'You mean that?'

'More than anything.' His hand clasped her arm. 'We're so good together—even Mr Jenkins agreed.'

'So we build a future based on an opinion poll of one patient?' Eyebrows peaking, she shook her head. 'That's not a lot to go on.'

'It's a start.'

'You haven't thought this through, Luke.'

'It's all I've done for five whole days.'

'And what about children? My work?'

'I haven't got all the answers. I just know I don't want this to end.' He pressed a kiss to her cheek and took her hand in his. 'Promise me you'll think about it.'

He made it sound so easy. It wasn't. She gave his hand a quick squeeze. 'Luke, one day you'll resent the fact I can't have kids. I've been there before, remember? Michael said he could cope. But he couldn't and he left. It's in every man's DNA, to further their genetic line.'

'Bloody Michael.' Luke's wonderful, hopeful face melted into a frown. A sneer flickered over his lips. 'I'm not like him.'

'No.' She reached a hand to Luke's cheek and stroked the beginnings of his five-o'clock stubble. 'No, you're not like Michael at all.'

Luke wanted her to stay. Hadn't been fazed by her infertility. Had asked her. 'And Lucy?'

'She'd love you to stay. I know she's not Charlotte, and no one could ever replace her. But we could be a family. Just us.' He ran his fingertips across her cheek. 'My girls.'

Everything she'd ever wanted, really. The only thing. To love, to be loved. To belong.

Relief consumed her. A new future within her grasp. It was a whole new scary ride. Trusting, loving, letting go. Giving herself up to a future she'd never thought she could have. To be a mother, finally, after all the pain. To love a man who loved her back.

Her heart swelled and she smiled. It was like letting in the light after years of darkness. 'Then yes.'

He pressed closer, circling his hands round her waist and drawing her against him. His eyes shone with heat. 'Yes, you'll stay?'

'Yes, yes. I'll think about it.'

A hard hammering on the door had them turning swiftly to blink at the blackness outside.

Jess made out two figures. They rapped hard again. 'Hello? Hello. Quick. Help.'

'Stacey?' Jess snagged the door open to let her patient in. A man had his shoulder under one of Stacey's arms and her face was ashen. 'What's the matter?'

'I think I'm losing my baby.'

Oh, God. Cold dread snaked down her spine. 'Luke, give me a hand here.'

'Baby?' Luke shot Jess a look that simultaneously asked a million questions and offered help. He turned to Stacey and took her hand. 'Hey, let's find somewhere more comfortable. Colin, this way.' His voice radiated confident warmth. So in command. *Trust me.*

And they all seemed to. Jess wanted to. She wanted that more than anything, and she was sure as hell going to try. Even though it frightened the heck out of her.

The man nodded. 'Sure.'

Following behind, Jess controlled her palpitations and made a quick assessment. Stacey was able to walk, there was no blood staining her clothes. All she could do was hope.

'In here.' Luke opened the door of his consulting room and helped lay Stacey down on the examination couch. 'Okay, tell me what's happening.'

'I had some pain, down there.' She rubbed her hand across her abdomen. 'And I'm bleeding.'

'This pain. Can you describe it?'

'Dull, like cramping. It's gone now.' Her lip wobbled. 'I'm scared.'

'I know. It can be frightening.' As he spoke he wrapped a blood-pressure cuff around her arm and held her wrist. 'I'm just checking your vitals. You look a bit pale.'

A bit? Jess admired his stoical approach. The woman was deathly white, but she seemed to relax a little when Luke spoke to her.

She tried to sit up, but Jess placed a hand on her shoulder. 'Just try to stay calm, Stacey. We'll help you.'

A tear edged down the mum's translucent skin and she grabbed Jess's arm. 'Save my baby. Please.'

An echo of the words Jessie had used. A knife twisted in her gut, jagged deep into her. She held her hand to her mouth and squeezed the tears back. Breathing seemed impossible. *Her baby.*

She pulled herself together, dragged in oxygen. She could not get emotional at a time like this.

Take a leaf from Luke's book. Stoical. Clinical. 'Let's just see what's going on first.'

There was little medical science could do to save a threatened miscarriage at thirteen weeks. All they could offer was hope and support, but it was too early to tell Stacey that. She glanced over at Luke with a questioning rise of her eyebrows.

He nodded. 'BP's one-twenty over seventy. Pulse seventy-two.' No immediate danger to Stacey. Perhaps not even to the foetus. Stacey's *baby*.

'Good.' She stroked Stacey's arm. 'Your blood pressure's fine so the bleeding isn't causing your circulation any problems.' For now. 'Are you wearing a pad? Would you be able to show me what the blood loss is like?'

She ushered Luke and Colin out of the room and drew curtains round the bed so she could assess the extent of the bleeding.

Luke lingered at the door. 'Are you okay with this?' he whispered to Jess.

Ever the gentleman. Sweet. Touching. But she was a professional after all. She could be strong. And even brave. Her lips curled into a smile around her words. 'Holding it together. Go talk to Colin. I think he needs you. He's in shock too.'

A pad with a few teaspoons worth of blood and only a little more on pelvic examination told her the bleed had been brief. But that didn't mean there wouldn't be more.

'Bleeding and spotting is common in pregnancy, some people have it all the way to term and have healthy babies.' Trying not to sugar-coat this too much, Jessie gave her the flip side too, and watched hope slide into despair. 'Stacey, as you know there is a higher risk of losing a baby in the first trimester.'

Her patient nodded, biting down on her bottom lip. 'But I'm at thirteen weeks now.' Her voice was weak.

Again Jess remembered a similar conversation in a hospital ward. Morphine and pain blurred the full memory.

Her heart tumbled. This poor woman. Miscarriage might be common, but the effects of losing a baby linger so long. *For ever.* She took a deep breath. 'I can't say that you are having a miscarriage. But it is a real possibility.'

'What should I do?'

'Sometimes it's just a case of resting and waiting to see what happens. That's the hardest part.'

More fat tears rolled down Stacey's cheeks. 'I want my baby.'

'I know. I know. I understand, Stacey.' She gulped in air. Gulped in air. *Breathe.*

'Is it still alive? How would we know? Can't you do a scan?'

'We don't have the right equipment here. You'd have to go to the hospital for an ultrasound. I can send you to A and E or arrange an appointment for tomorrow.' Glancing over at the equipment cupboard in the corner, she grasped what slice of hope she could. 'But I could…try to find a heartbeat if you want?'

'And what if you can't?'

Jess regretted her words already. It was rash to raise Stacey's hopes. But in her situation she'd grab whatever slim hope there was. Had done. 'Then it doesn't mean the baby's lost. It means I can't find it with the probe. Often we can't hear the heartbeat until after fourteen weeks, sixteen for some. Look, Stacey, a proper scan would be better.'

The woman's fist closed over Jessie's. 'Do it. Do it now.'

'Luke can I have a word?' Jessie called down the corridor, and felt relief wash over her as he strode towards her.

'You okay, babe?' His eyes darted over her face and he palmed her cheek. 'This must be hard for you.'

Her mouth was dry. She hadn't realised, but now

she was out of the room her hands were shaking. 'I'm fine. I'm going to try a Doppler.'

'Are you sure?'

'I've found them at thirteen weeks before. She's desperate.'

'I just looked at her notes. Now I understand what all that pregnancy-test business was about on your first day. I was so confused. You were protecting her.'

Pushing her hair back from her forehead, he pressed a kiss to her frown. It gave her courage. God knew, she needed it.

'Give the Doppler a whirl. Should I bring Colin in?'

'Absolutely. She could do with all the support she can get. And me too.'

As Jess squirted jelly onto Stacey's tummy Colin sat by the couch with his head in his hands. 'I didn't even know you were pregnant. If I had, I'd have watched over you better. Been more…been there.'

'It's okay.' Stacey clasped her husband's hand. 'I didn't want to tell you. I was scared of what might happen between us.'

The dad ran her knuckles across his mouth. 'Is miscarriage caused by stress?'

Trying to get the Doppler in the right position, Jess paused and listened. Nothing.

The shaking wouldn't stop, which wasn't helping. She willed her hands to still and prayed to whatever spirit out there would listen. *Stacey needs this baby.*

Luke held his breath then exhaled slowly. Maybe this wasn't going to be one of the lucky ones. He sat and looked at Colin on the other side of the bed. Poor guy, just found he's going to be a dad. And then had it snatched away from him. Judging by the look on his face, he thought it was his fault.

'No, Colin. There are lots of reasons why miscarriages happen. Mostly it's just nature's way.'

'It's just…I've been an idiot, Stace. Trying to lay down the law without listening. I'm going to be there for you from now on. And for Kyle. And this baby.'

Luke tried to imagine what it would have been like to have lost Lucy. Hell, he couldn't go there. Couldn't fathom what that must feel like. But Stacey and Colin were going through it now. Jessie had lived through it and the ramifications pretty much on her own. And here she was, watching an action replay but holding it together like a true professional. A survivor. Yet the slope of her shoulders and the trembling of her hand gave her emotion away. At least to him, anyway.

'Do you want me to have a go?' He slid next to her and put his hand on top of hers, held the Doppler with her. He felt her relax slightly against him, the trembling abating.

A slight tilt of the probe, and a twist towards where he imagined a baby's heart to be. Damn it, he was running blind. 'Sometimes it's just a matter of getting the angle right.'

Together they held their breath.

Still nothing.

Jessie looked up at him. Dark shadows bruised her eyes, her mouth formed a tight line. She shook her head.

'Just another go, eh?' He was not going to give this up. Not for Stacey or Colin. Or Jess. 'How about here?'

Another tweak, a tilt and slight pressure. No one spoke.

No one breathed.

And then…a flicker, and another, and another. The feathery *fwap-fwap-fwap* of a tiny heart. Not yet fourteen weeks but there. *There.*

'Is that…?' Stacey tried to sit up again and the Doppler slipped. The sound faded. 'Was it?'

A shock of relief made Jess's legs wobble. A

heartbeat. A growing, viable baby. She gripped the side of the couch and watched the thrill on everyone's faces. Stacey, not out of the woods yet but making her way, had a huge smile on her tear-stained face. Colin looked bemused, shocked and proud. So very proud.

And Luke. Beautiful, handsome Luke beaming almost as much as Colin and looking equally delighted. Without his help she wouldn't have found that heartbeat. His steady hand and courage had pushed them to find what she hadn't been able to.

All sounds in the room seemed to die away as she watched him smiling at Colin.

Only a few minutes ago he'd asked her stay.

How could she? How could she deprive him of what Colin had? The promise of a new life, a future, a new beginning.

A wretched ache closed her throat and the walls closed in. Luke was standing too close, his hand still covering hers. His heat and strength diffused into her. She had a choice. Lean against him and feel the comfort and security he offered. Or walk away.

The reality of what that meant made her heart almost break.

She tried to laugh and smile along with the others, pretended the tears spilling down her cheeks were ones of joy.

She hugged the mum-to-be. 'Yes! We all heard it, didn't we?'

Colin nodded and looked away.

Luke stared at his feet, his throat too thick with emotion to utter a word.

He dealt with this kind of thing every day and yet today, sharing it with Jess, had been incredible. His heart felt like it was going to jump out of his chest at the thought that they'd be sharing so much more from now on.

Once they'd waved the relieved couple away, with strict instructions to rest up and call if they were worried, Jess and Luke were left alone again in the surgery.

Jess finished tidying up and watched as Luke closed down the computer and straightened the blinds on the window. A guilty smile hovered on his lips. He raised an eyebrow and she too remembered the passionate kiss before Stacey and Colin had arrived. *Just one kiss.*

'That was intense,' she said to him. 'Thanks, by the way. I don't know if I'd have managed to find that heartbeat without you.'

'Sure you would. It just took a bit of time.' He

put his arm round her shoulder and squeezed tight. 'You ready to come home?'

Home. She had no idea where that was.

But it wasn't here. What she'd witnessed earlier had muddied her determination. 'Think I'll hang around here a bit.'

'Told you we're a good team.'

'We didn't exactly do anything. Stacey wasn't in danger. That baby was safe all along.' He wasn't hearing her. She edged from his arms and realised she was jittery. And cold. She needed to be on her own for a while to think.

'But she came to us. That's all we can ask for, Jess—patients who trust us. She trusts you.'

She opened the door for him. 'It's getting late, Luke. Go home to Lucy. I'll see you later, tomorrow.'

Summer heat blasted through to the air-conditioned room. He glanced outside, then back at Jess. Then it seemed to hit him.

He'd heard, he just hadn't wanted to. Or he'd just figured it out. A shadow crossed his face. 'Jess… about before…'

'Go, Luke. I need to think.'

It was late when Jess walked down the cul-de-sac to the fanfare of chirruping cicadas. The humid air hung heavily on her skin. Beads of sweat trickled down her back.

She'd walked long and hard, watched the ocean dip and flow. And made her decision.

Tonight and tomorrow stretched ahead like an unmarked path. But at least she knew where she'd be on Saturday.

'I was worried about you.'

On his front step, Luke sat hunched against the porch door, illuminated by the intruder light. A million moths dived wildly around the glowing beam like shooting stars. A bottle of beer hung from his hand. Now, just as the first time she'd seen him in full focus, right here in this spot, her heart stuttered.

Of course he was waiting for her. That was the wonderful thing about Luke, he always did the right thing. Taking in Chloe even though he hadn't really known her. Asking *her* to stay even when she couldn't bear him children. When, *when* would he get what he wanted?

He walked towards her, opened the gate and beckoned her through. 'Where've you been?'

'Walking, thinking.' Her resolve stumbled. She could do this. He would thank her when he had a wife and a horde of little McKenzies. She needed to tell him now before she lost her nerve. 'I'm going to Dunedin. I'm leaving. For good.'

The vibrancy and vitality seemed to be sucked out of him. 'Why?'

'Because I have to. This…us…can't happen.'

He pulled her to sit next to him on the warm step. 'Sure it can, babe. If we want it to.'

She edged just out of his reach. She could do this. She could walk away. She had to. But she couldn't touch him. 'You're amazing, Luke. Everything here is amazing. But I'm too scared, I have to go.'

'Scared of what, Jess?'

'Of losing everything. Of being hurt again.'

'I won't hurt you.'

Knowing I can't have you already hurts too much. 'I want to believe you.' It was so hard to explain, how much she wanted him but how much it would be better for them both if she left.

'I just watched the joy and pride in Colin's face as he stroked Stacey's stomach. And I want you to have that. You didn't see Chloe's belly swell, feel the flutter of kicks against your palm, experience your baby growing from a strawberry to a lime to a grapefruit, and you deserve to have that—as many siblings for Lucy as you want.'

'I don't care about any of that. I want you.'

'And I want you, Luke, but I can't ask you to give

that all up. One day, when you think you've dealt with not having it, you'll want it so badly you'll resent me.' Her voice had cracked but she was holding it together. No tears. Yet. Good. 'And I can't risk loving you then losing you. I've lost too much already. I don't think I could recover from that.'

'I wouldn't swap a lifetime with you for another baby.' His voice became animated. 'Stay, Jess. Be my wife, and Lucy's mum.'

'I can't.'

'You won't, you mean. Damn right you're scared. I am too.'

His face filled with anger and frustration, his jaw taut and his eyes flared with hurt. 'The last time I asked a woman to stay she managed nine months. You think I want that to happen again?'

'No.'

'But I can spend my life being scared or take a risk.' He paused. 'I love you.'

'Oh, Luke.' It was a swift punch to the chest. A wonderful, painful thump that whooshed out her breath. Her heart thundered against her ribcage. She willed it to slow. She couldn't let him persuade her and then blame her later for the end of his dreams. 'You can't love me.'

'I know.' He laughed and shook his head. 'It's against every rule in my book. But I do. You're mad and unpredictable and downright crazy. You're great with Lucy too. She loves you. *I* love you.'

He saw her wince as he mentioned his daughter's name. Damn stubborn woman. It was Chloe all over again. Only she wasn't Chloe, she was so much more than that. Chloe had been selfish and uncompromising.

Whereas Jess…Jess believed she was doing the right thing for him. And she was hurting as much as he was. Maybe she just needed time to get used to the idea. But they didn't have time, and he got the feeling that if she left she'd just keep on going. 'You're brave, Jess. We can do this together. Stay.'

'I'm not brave, Luke. You just want me to be.' She palmed his cheek. 'You know, you and I are very similar. We both have life plans. Yours is to be planned and ordered, mine is to run. I get that now. All those years in Asia, I wasn't trying to find a vocation, I was running. Scared and alone. But that's okay. The nature of the job means I get to keep moving on, it's what I've always done. It fits.'

'You want it to fit because you're too scared to do anything else.'

She stood up and inhaled deeply. She would not allow him to persuade her, no matter how much she regretted this. 'I'm going, Luke. Nothing you can say or do is going to change my mind.'

'What we have is amazing. Have you ever felt like this before?'

'No.' It came out like a moan. How could such a short word be so painful?

'Do you love me?'

'Love you? I don't know.' Everything in her heart screamed *yes*. How could she not love him? 'I think so.'

'You *think* so? Not good enough.' He stood. Cupping her chin, he looked deep into her eyes, reached down into her soul and tugged. Hard. 'Do. You. Love. Me?'

'I…' She blinked and swept a hand across her face. *I won't say it, and make this so much more difficult.*

'You love me. I can see it, Jess. You're transparent remember? Your eyes tell me, your face tells me. Every time you look at me I see that connection. But you want to pretend it isn't there.'

'I'm going to Dunedin.' Moving her chin from his hand, she tried to turn her back on him. Stupid legs wouldn't work. First her heart and now her body was rebelling against her. *Come on, give me a chance here.* 'It's better this way. No one gets hurt.'

'You think? You're not hurting now?' He grasped her arms in his hands. Never had he looked more fervent, more devastating. 'If you're too frightened to take a chance on love then, hell, I don't know what more I can do. Jessie, it's your loss.'

'It is. I know. You're a good man and I know what I'm leaving, believe me. I'm sorry. I truly am.'

Her facial muscles seemed to want to contort themselves. Tears threatened. She blinked them away. Caught a rogue one before it ran down her cheek. Any second now she was going to cave in.

But she allowed herself one more kiss. Brushed her lips against the cool skin of his cheek and inhaled his spicy scent. Tried to lock the taste and the feel of him deep in her heart to take out in the dark moments and treasure.

'Hey, at least this way we can look back and remember we had an amazing time, Luke. It was only ever perfect.'

CHAPTER TWELVE

IF SHE'D thought last week had been hard, trying to keep her distance from Luke, then every second of Friday speared Jess like a knife.

It was over. It was messy and it hurt like hell. Her heart would never be the same. Any hope of a painless end was impossible.

But she could walk away knowing she'd done the right thing by them all. Now she just had to get through one more day.

'You on a fitness campaign or something?' Maggie asked when Jess went running over the lunch hour. Just to keep away from him.

She'd hoped that keeping busy would help, but it just exhausted her. She spent the evening swimming endless lengths in the pool, but that only made her think of Luke, and green hair and stolen kisses in the kitchen.

And at night, alone in the dark, when sleep wouldn't come, she went over and over and over it all. Tried to get his face out of her mind, tried to erase the smell of him on her skin. But nothing worked.

If she'd thought that setting him free would make life easier, she had been sorely mistaken.

She'd willingly trade every second of that lonely freedom for just one minute in his arms or one final kiss, even a tender glance. But it would get them nowhere, however tempting it was to just walk across the road and into his bed.

And the sight of little Lucy waving forlornly from the garden as Jess jogged home almost broke her heart.

What were the chances of Lucy understanding what was going on when the adults didn't?

Roll on tomorrow, and her flight to Dunedin. Then there'd be something to look forward to. At least, that's what she was trying to convince herself.

Luke sat in his study and watched the light in Jess's bedroom go out. The inability to *do* anything frustrated the hell out of him.

She was leaving and there was nothing he could do about it, short of dragging her into his bed and holding her prisoner. Which, although delicious and very tempting, was probably illegal in a million different ways.

Damned stubborn woman.

He'd hoped he'd shouted some sense into her. Made her realise what she was throwing away. But no.

It was her loss, he'd said. But it was his too. A deep, tangible, painful loss.

Now he was all out of ideas. All out of trying to convince yet another woman to stay.

They were definitely, definitely off the menu from now.

A small whimper came from Lucy's bedroom. Then a cough.

He looked away from the window, from the lost hope in that house across the road. Then he stood, turned out the light and went to tend to his little girl.

The journey to the airport took longer than usual. Roadworks meant a detour through the city centre. Past the Magic Planet entrance. Past the play park.

Clutching the car seat, Jess watched Auckland whiz by and tried to eradicate the memories and images of Luke whirling in her head. *It will be better in Dunedin without so many reminders.*

Sheesh, better in Dunedin? She was a walking, talking scrapbook of emotions and experiences. As if a few thousand kilometres would make things better.

She paid the taxi, scanned her phone for messages and checked in quickly. Twenty minutes to kill before boarding usually meant a shopping opportunity, but she lacked the interest or the desire to waste her money on trinkets.

She flicked through magazines at the newsagent's, checked her phone again. Drank a trim milk latte and checked her phone some more.

'What are you hoping for, Jess?' she asked herself, as she scanned the tiny screen for the millionth time. 'Why would he text at all?'

It was no use. She couldn't go without saying goodbye. One last call to wish him well.

Okay, so you want to hear his voice. Admit it.

I want to hear his voice.

Straight to the answering-machine.

She didn't leave a message. Didn't know what to say. Her throat thickened. *Well, at least you heard his voice, Jess, my girl.*

Jess. Her heart kicked at the thought of it. At what point had she stopped being Jessie and become Jess? At what point had she started seeing herself the way he saw her, the way Lucy wanted her to be?

He'd changed her. They'd changed her. Made her believe she was beautiful, something good. Made her believe, for a moment, that anything could be possible.

Take a chance, he'd said.

And she'd walked away. Too scared to try again. Too scared of being hurt, of not being able to love.

But who was she kidding? She hurt just the same. Worse, because she'd lost love all over again.

Luke and Lucy had been willing to accept her for who and what she was, and what she couldn't be. But she'd spurned that. Chosen to run away from the chance of love.

Giving her heart to him was scary, but living without him terrified her.

A kernel of hope, a tiny nugget of gold, glowed in the pit of her stomach. Maybe it was time to do what he said. Maybe it was time to start living.

Start loving?

She realised, then, with a striking blow, that she really did love him absolutely and hopelessly. A deep, earthly love that tied her to him, to his daughter and to this place. A love that even geography couldn't kill. A love she was tired of hiding from.

Had she blown her chance with him?

Would he even listen to her?

She tried his phone again. Suddenly she needed to hear his voice. Not wanted, needed.

Boarding now.

Or she could walk down that concourse and get on the plane. Her courage wobbled. What if he turned her away?

Then she'd go on living. She could do that. They'd given her a gift of self-belief. She'd learnt so much from him and his beautiful little girl about life, about fun and about love.

Just one more try. His home phone this time. It was early, he probably wasn't up yet.

No answer.

'Why aren't you there? Luke, where are you?'

Last call.

She glanced hopefully around the departure lounge.

Then laughed at herself. As if he'd be here. This wasn't a romantic film, he wouldn't be here with balloons and flowers. She'd already spurned him enough.

He wasn't at the airport. He wasn't home. So where was he at seven o'clock in the morning?

The house was deserted. Heart pounding in her chest, Jess ran back down the path to the waiting taxi. Damn it, she'd been in enough cars today to last her for the next month. 'Take me to North Beach hospital…I think.'

It was the only answer. He wasn't returning her calls or texts. Lucy must have been taken in again. Asthma. *God, no*. Lucy needed her. Luke needed her to help with the nebs. He was hopeless at singing.

What should she do? Sit and wait? Or go to the only place she imagined them to be.

The taxi pulled away from the kerb and slowly edged up the hill towards the main road. Jess scanned behind for signs of her family.

Her family. *His girls*. She wanted to be one of them—if he'd have her. If it wasn't too late. Her heart thumped as she realised what a stupid fool she'd been. She loved him, loved them both, but hadn't told them. And what if now…it was too late?

Her throat closed over. No, she couldn't think such terrible things. Lucy would be fine. She would be.

Just before the car reached the intersection a familiar figure toddled round the corner.

'Stop! Now.' She hauled out of the car and thrust way too much cash at the driver, who stared at her and left her luggage on the pavement. 'Lucy! Come here.'

'Jess! Jess.' Jessie's heart melted, along with the rest of her. The little mite was dressed head to toe in a pink and white polka-dot bikini with matching floppy hat and sparkly jandals. A pink swim ring snuggled around her midriff and she clutched a red bucket and spade. 'We been to the beach.'

'At seven o'clock?'

A chubby, hot hand fitted into Jess's, and she grasped it tightly. *Never let me go.*

'Daddy builded sandcastles.'

'Good old Daddy.' *I'm going to kill him.* 'Where is he?'

Her phone rang. 'Luke?'

'Jess? I've a million missed calls from you. Where are you? What is it?' His voice boomed towards her as he rounded the corner, relaxed and gorgeous in his board shorts and flip-flops.

'Jess.' Softer now, warm, velvet soft. He flipped his phone away. His smile was curious and uncertain. She hated that she'd made him unsure, that he wavered, doubted their connection. 'You came back.'

His bare torso rippled as he closed the distance between them, a sheen of silver-black volcanic sand covering him. She let her hand slip out of Lucy's and reached to him. Her breath hitched in her chest. Just like the first time she'd seen him. Like every time she saw him. *Never stop feeling like this.*

Then she swatted his arm. 'Never ever scare me

like that again, d'you hear? I thought she was in hospital. I was worried to death. Do you know how many car journeys I've had to make today? Two. Long ones. And I was just about to take another one to the hospital. I was scared, Luke. Scared to come back, scared to see you, scared about Lucy. And you were *playing* at the beach? Never let me feel like that again. Never. Again.'

'Welcome home, dear. Neither of us could sleep so we took an early morning walk.' He smiled and rubbed his arm playfully. Then his eyes blazed intense steel grey. 'Why are you here, Jess?'

'I…'

She'd planned exactly what she was going to say, but words failed her. Just looking into his magnificent face, mussy from lack of sleep, dark shadows under his eyes, made her breathless. She could feel the words, but couldn't find them. 'I…'

'Because I need you to be honest. Truly, truly honest, Jess.' He drew her away out of Lucy's earshot. 'I won't let you hurt her. Or me. You hear? We deserve better. So if you're not going to stay forever then you might as well go now. Get that plane to Dunedin.'

'I don't want to go to Dunedin.'

'Why not?'

'Because you're not in Dunedin. You're here, and that's where I want to be. With you. I love you.'

There, she'd said it. Risked her heart, her everything. And now she'd said it once it rolled off her tongue. Easy. Easy to let love in once you took a risk. 'I love you, Luke McKenzie.'

'I know, you fool.' He laughed and shook his head. 'I knew it when we made love. I've known it a long time. Shame you haven't.'

'Hush.' She put a hand to his mouth, felt the soft line of his lips under her fingers. *Kiss me.* 'Lucy will hear.'

'I don't care who hears. I love you, Jess. More than anything.'

Tears welled in her eyes, and she let them fall. 'But what about babies? Lucy needs brothers and sisters.'

'We'll work it out, there's always a way. The main thing is, loving each other, loving Lucy, being a family.'

'Well, we can certainly do that. There's a bucketful of love here, Luke.' She touched a hand to her heart. 'A whole universe worth for you and for Lucy.'

'And any others we might have.'

'Of course.' She swallowed a lump in her throat,

wiped her tears with her sleeve and laughed. 'Just how many did you have in mind?'

'Oh, a couple, or five.' He grinned. 'Come here.'

Then his mouth was on hers, claiming her as his, and she gave herself up to him, laughing and kissing and smiling. The familiar dangerous glint in his eye reminded her what kind of loving he had in mind.

'Five?' She pulled away, not far, because she didn't ever want to be apart from him again, but enough that she could see his face. 'Five?'

'Yep. And a chicken. Or really? Just the one if that's all we're lucky enough to have.' He grinned down at her and she saw the love shining in his eyes. 'I love you, Jess.'

'I know.'

And she did. It felt so good to be in his arms, in his life, in his future.

EPILOGUE

Two years later...

'IT'S a boy!' Jess cradled the phone to her chest and grinned. 'A boy.'

Another one.

When the heck was it going to stop? Luke clearly hadn't been joking when he'd said he wanted five kids. Her heart swelled. *Thank goodness.*

She couldn't imagine another life now. Didn't want one.

She rapped on the kitchen window to get their attention as they whizzed past. No such luck.

Why stop and listen when you're having fun?

Three little heads bobbed up from a wheelbarrow then turned into a spaghetti of arms and legs as they tumbled and wriggled. Luke pushed the barrow, chatting to her brother Zac, their heads tipped back in fits of laughter. Luke's stride, as always, was steady and purposeful, but he'd made fun into an art form.

Following the screams and giggles, she found

them in the chicken coop with Lucy, Angel and Tom gathering eggs for lunch.

'I just had a call from Julie at Social Services. It's another boy.' She ruffled their two-year-old son's black curls and he wriggled under her touch. She inhaled the soft, earthy fragrance of boy. Her heart stuttered. He was so vibrant and alive. Adorable. 'So we'll have two of each. Just perfect.'

'Yes, two cheeky monkeys and two little monsters.' Luke tickled Angel, their ever-so-serious adopted five-year-old Vietnamese daughter, and her face split into a grin.

Even after two years Jess was surprised at how much overwhelmingly fierce love she had for her adopted children, and yet could still find more for foster-kids that passed through their lives. 'He's a tot. Only nine months, so you'd better lift the baby gear down from the loft.'

'Will do.'

'I'll give you a hand.' Zac wrapped an arm round Jessie's shoulder. 'Well done, sis.'

'Thanks.' She pecked him a kiss on the cheek. Never in her lifetime had she thought they'd both end up settled. *In the same place.* Despite their difficult upbringing, they'd managed to put roots down together. It was amazing what healing a little loving could do. Although she still had to find him a wife.

She hugged him close. 'More babysitting duties for their favourite uncle?'

'We've got to wet the baby's head first. Tradition.' Luke nodded and smiled. 'Nine months? Separation anxiety stage, huh? Be prepared. I'm warning you, it's not pretty. What's his story?'

She steered him out of the children's earshot. 'Parents killed in a car crash. Desperately sad. They're looking for long-term fostering, with a view to adoption. The paperwork will take some time, I think. We'll just have to wait and see. Very sad for the little tyke.'

'It always is, Jess.' He pulled her against his chest and hugged her tight. 'But no regrets?'

'On giving up the overseas charity work? Not on your life. Our kids need us.'

'Almost as much as we need them.'

They strolled back up to the kitchen door arm in arm. Then, while he removed his gumboots, she looked through to the jumble of washing, the art wall of pictures that still looked like sperm caught in tornadoes.

Their wedding photo sat amongst the many framed photos on the shelves, of Luke and herself and Lucy, their flower-girl. The wedding reception at the Magic Planet—because, hey, it was the perfect venue.

Jess's heart snagged as she caught sight of the little black and white snap of Charlotte's twenty-week scan. As Luke's arms wrapped round her waist, the sound of her children's laughter in her ears, she blew her baby a kiss. 'I love you, baby, to the moon and back.'

Even though she'd missed the chance of having her own child, she was so grateful for all this chaos and joy in her life, for her family. For the chance to be a mother.

More than anything, she was thankful for the constant love of her darling husband. She wriggled round in his arms, pressed her lips against his, enjoyed the heat of his body against hers, and the promise of a lifetime of love. 'No Luke, no regrets.'

* * * * *

Mills & Boon® Large Print Medical

October

November

December

Mills & Boon® Large Print
Medical

January

SYDNEY HARBOUR HOSPITAL: MARCO'S TEMPTATION	Fiona McArthur
WAKING UP WITH HIS RUNAWAY BRIDE	Louisa George
THE LEGENDARY PLAYBOY SURGEON	Alison Roberts
FALLING FOR HER IMPOSSIBLE BOSS	Alison Roberts
LETTING GO WITH DR RODRIGUEZ	Fiona Lowe
DR TALL, DARK...AND DANGEROUS?	Lynne Marshall

February

SYDNEY HARBOUR HOSPITAL: AVA'S RE-AWAKENING	Carol Marinelli
HOW TO MEND A BROKEN HEART	Amy Andrews
FALLING FOR DR FEARLESS	Lucy Clark
THE NURSE HE SHOULDN'T NOTICE	Susan Carlisle
EVERY BOY'S DREAM DAD	Sue MacKay
RETURN OF THE REBEL SURGEON	Connie Cox

March

HER MOTHERHOOD WISH	Anne Fraser
A BOND BETWEEN STRANGERS	Scarlet Wilson
ONCE A PLAYBOY...	Kate Hardy
CHALLENGING THE NURSE'S RULES	Janice Lynn
THE SHEIKH AND THE SURROGATE MUM	Meredith Webber
TAMED BY HER BROODING BOSS	Joanna Neil